Resting on his heels, Saint brushed his sopping orange hair off his muddy forehead. He frowned over at the computer terminal that floated in the air near the trunk of a squat palm tree.

"One does hope, old thing, you're not a minion of the law."

"I'm Whistler," explained the voxbox of the terminal. "Representing the Whistler Interplanetary Investigation Agency."

Saint shook off his dripping sleeves. "Come to arrest me, have you?"

"Nope, we want to hire you."

"To do an honest job, do you mean?"

"Exactly."

"Jove," said Saint thoughtfully as he rose, dripping, to his feet, "I may have sunk low enough to take you up on that."

SUICIDE, Inc.

RON GOULART

BERKLEY BOOKS, NEW YORK

SUICIDE, INC.

A Berkley Book / published by arrangement with
the author

PRINTING HISTORY
Berkley edition / March 1985

ISBN: 0-425-07586-9

A BERKLEY BOOK® TM 757,375
Berkley Books are published by The Berkley Publishing Group,
200 Madison Avenue, New York, New York 10016.
The name ''BERKLEY'' and the stylized ''B'' with design are
trademarks belonging to Berkley Publishing Corporation.
PRINTED IN THE UNITED STATES OF AMERICA

1 ═══════════════

Smith was recruited first.

That was in an alley.

The alley was narrow and quirky, thick with misty shadows and rich with foul smells. It angled along behind a nameless saloon and dead-ended against a mildew-streaked brix wall. This particular alley was in Deadzone 22 in the capital city of the largest territory on the planet Barnum, but Jared Smith had encountered similar problems in other alleys all across the Barnum System and elsewhere during the past twelve or thirteen months.

The specific problem in the Deadzone 22 alley consisted of a large broadshouldered catman, an even huskier lizardman and a crackbeaked scarlet birdman, who was both smaller and nastier than his companions. All three had taken exception to Smith while inside the murky saloon, and had suggested stepping out here to settle their differences.

Smith had been drinking mulled skullpop, a powerful mix of alcohol, euphorium and propolis. A long lanky man of thirty-one, he'd found he was incapable of ignoring challenges much beyond the third drink. Even challenges from huge hulking louts near twice his present lean weight.

"Making snide remarks about the blasted zither player, were you?" grunted the catman, who was a muddy brindle color, as he commenced knocking Smith against the slimy brix of the alley wall. "This'll teach you to keep your gob shut."

"Merely mentioned," explained Smith, bouncing back and getting in two quick jabs to the catman's furry midsection, "that the fellow was a mite heavy-clawed."

"He's the best damn lobsterman zither player in this corner of the universe, mate." The lizardman joined in the fracas, accompanying his comment with a smart kick to Smith's ribs.

Losing his balance, Smith fell to one knee in the sticky purplish muck that paved the twisting alley.

Before he could rise again the bouncy birdman got a claw around his neck. "Let's scruff him."

"Not yet," growled the catman. "I wants to batter the bastard around some more first."

"Aw, a bloody waste of time." The birdman produced a wicked sawtooth gutting knife with the claw that wasn't throttling Smith. "I'm going to slice his gullet right . . . crikey!"

A flurry of scarlet feathers came exploding down on Smith.

The birdman was no longer clutching him. Instead he was crumpled up way down at the dark end of the alley, eyes shut, beak quivering.

"Where do you get off stunning our pal?" The catman was snarling at the compact computer terminal that had appeared all at once a few feet away.

It was floating in the thick, sour air about four feet above the ground.

Smith had the impression that a thin yellow beam of light had come shooting from the newly arrived gadget, hit the birdman and flipped him aside. "That's an interesting trick," he muttered while struggling to rise out of the muck.

"I'll teach you!" The lizardman snatched a lazgun from beneath his tunic, and swung the barrel toward the floating terminal.

"Twerp," remarked the gadget's voxbox.

The beam this time was an intense throbbing green. It took the charging lout in the chest, lifted him clear off the ground, then tossed him atop his fallen comrade.

Smith was standing again, but swaying, watching all this through narrowed bloodshot eyes. He blinked, rubbed at his stubbled chin and took a couple of breaths through his open mouth.

"We was merely having a little musical discussion," the catman informed the formidable terminal. "No need, chum, for you to come materializing out of bloody nowhere to bap my mates. Fact is, I bet our insurance attorney can sue you for—"

"Scram," suggested the terminal, its screen turning an ominous black.

"Okay, okay, so much for free speech in this swill hole." Hunching his wide shoulders, the catman went stomping toward the mouth of the alley. He scowled back at Smith. "Might just be, pal, that we'll continue our conversation sometime when your blooming buddy ain't around." Growling, he walked off.

"He's no friend of . . ." Smith paused, realizing that he was feeling pretty dizzy.

"Jared Smith, isn't it?" The terminal came floating

closer to him, bouncing on the twilight air.

"Sure, that's who . . . I am." He swallowed a few times. "These damn workouts . . . take a lot out of . . ." He dropped, once again, to his knees.

The terminal sighed. "I wonder, Smith, if you're even worth trying to salvage."

"Salvage?" He toppled over, landing face first in the muck.

It was raining where he awakened.

A thin, quiet rain drifting straight down out of the night sky. The rain hit, softly, on the plaz dome roof of the room Smith found himself in.

He sat, carefully, up on the oval airbed.

Interestingly enough, the dimlit room did not go spinning around. Smith had been waking up like that a lot lately. This time was different. And his head, now that he thought about it, didn't ache either. Didn't throb, didn't give him the unpleasant impression that his brain was expanding and contracting inside his skull.

Bringing his hand up to scratch his chin, Smith discovered he no longer had his week-old collection of stubble decorating his weatherbeaten, slightly battered face. He noticed, too, that his left arm ached at a spot midway between shoulder and elbow.

"Bastards gave me some kind of shot." He swung off the bed, planting his bare feet on the thick thermorug.

What bastards exactly? Frowning, Smith made his way across the shadowy circular room and slumped down into a spunglaz slingchair. He concentrated on remembering.

"Fracas in the alley . . . catman . . . birdman . . . who the hell was the third one? . . . Robot, wasn't it? . . . Right, he fouled me with a tin fist in the crotch and . . .

nope, wait. . . . That robot was someplace else . . . last month out on—''

''Tarragon.''

''Yep, right. The planet was Tarragon. He was a big, clunky . . . hey!'' Smith stood, spinning to face the small computer terminal.

It was floating at chest level a few feet away from him. ''In your most recent senseless brawl, Smitty, your third opponent was a lizardman.''

''How do you know?''

''Wasn't I there?''

Smith took a step toward it. ''Sure, I remember. You saved me the trouble of decking that trio of halfwits.''

''And saved them the fun of stomping you into the muck.''

''Like hell. I was winning on points when you came barging in to—''

''Sit down.''

''Another thing.'' He pointed down at his bare feet. ''Did you swipe my boots?''

''They went down the dispozhole while you snoozed,'' replied the terminal's voxbox. ''Being judged too foul to salvage.''

''C'mon, I paid nearly five hundred trubux for those out on Tarragon only a few—''

''Groutcrap. You swiped them off a drunken snergherder in a flophouse on the planet Esmeralda six months ago,'' the floating terminal informed him. ''To the abundance of snergdroppings already encrusting the footwear you've since added—''

''Okay, but what about the shot in the arm?''

''That was intended to sober you up. Which it appears nearly to have done. Sit down. You can call me Whistler.''

Smith, reluctantly, sat again in the slingchair. ''Why

exactly have you . . . whoa now!" He popped to his feet, pointing an accusing finger at the gadget. "That's Whistler as in Whistler Interplanetary Investigation Agency, isn't it?"

"Very perceptive, Smitty."

"I don't want to have a damn thing to do with you guys," Smith told Whistler. "Thanks for lending me a hand in that frumus, and, if you can hustle me up some new boots, I'll bid you fond farewell and go on about my—"

"Afraid to work for us?"

Smith shook his head. "Listen, my foolhardy days are a long time over." He glanced around for a way out. "I've done some risky jobs, but I'm not dim or desperate enough yet to go to work for the Whistler Agency. You must know the nickname your outfit has all across the—"

"Suicide, Inc.," replied the floating terminal. "Nice zing to it, but it's an exaggeration. We aren't foolhardy either, far from it, and we've never undertaken any job that promised to be completely—"

"Suicide, Inc. Sure, you heartless sons of bitches send operatives and investigators out to the worst pestholes in the Barnum System," Smith accused. "And even to the planets in the Hellquad and—"

"The Trinidad System, too."

Smith sat. "Anyway, I don't intend to take a job with you guys," he said. "If that's what the kidnapping was all about."

The night rain hit gently on the roof. A soft wind rattled unseen tree branches and foliage out in the surrounding dark.

"You were born on the planet Zegundo in the Trinidads," said Whistler.

"Far as I know." He shifted in the chair. "I'd just as well not talk about that."

"You grew up in the Selva Territory, at a place called Horizon House," continued the terminal. "That was a shelter for displaced children who—"

"Who is the real Whistler anyway? You guys call yourself the Whistler Agency, yet nobody seems to know for certain if Whistler's a person, an android or just a computer who—"

"Not important," cut in the Whistler terminal. "Has nothing at all to do with the problem we want you to—"

"What I want to do is exit." He rose, slowly, to his feet. "You going to let me?"

"Not just yet, no."

"I won't," he reiterated, "work for Suicide, Inc."

"You served two years with the Interplan Law Service, then three with the Political Espionage Office," said Whistler. "That was after coming here from the Trinidad System, where you'd worked in the Territorial Police in Selva."

"And even earlier I used to play with toy rockets and skycars," said Smith. "But I've grown older since, it happens to most everybody, and given up a lot of youthful crap."

"You were an exceptional lawman and investigator," said the terminal, "until about two years ago."

"I keep getting older. I just matured to the point where I no longer saw any sense to any of it."

"Was it because of that incident out on Peregrine or was it because of the marriage of—"

"Wasn't any one thing." He took some steps in the direction of the door he'd spotted.

"Do you really enjoy your present life?"

Smith laughed. "You are versatile," he observed,

grinning. "You can teleport yourself into alleys, cold-cock rowdies *and* deliver sermons. Terrific."

"We happen to have, Smith, an assignment you're suited for."

"Nope, no. You don't."

"But in order to handle it, and boss the crew we're putting together, you have to be sober," the terminal told him. "And you have to be willing to go back to Zegundo."

Smith watched Whistler for several silent seconds. "Tell me," he requested finally, "some more about the job."

2

Cruz was already out in the Trinidad System when the Whistler Agency approached him.

He was way up in the bell tower of a glaz and metal cathedral, concentrating on holding off an irate husband who was intent on doing him several kinds of bodily harm. Unfortunately, Cruz, a large, dark man of thirty-five, had left his right arm downstairs in the stark white bedchamber of the wife of the Most Reverend Charles Waldenbrook. So he was forced to defend himself one-handed and with only the dinky stungun he'd managed to grab from the lovely young Mrs. Waldenbrook's purse as he went hurrying out the window.

This was in the heart of Metropolis Territory's second largest city, on the planet Primero. It was midway through a hazy Sunday morning.

"You sure better get all this folderol taken care of by eleven," warned the small roundshouldered birdman who sat hunched over the console of the tower musicizer. "My eleven o'clock bell concert is the real high-point of the day and I don't want any distractions."

Cruz was crouching behind a huge imitation bell that sat on the plaz flooring of the open air tower. Some fifteen yards away Reverend Waldenbrook could be seen peering around the half-open neowood door to the stairwell. He held a stungun in his left hand, a lazgun in his right and a kilgun between his teeth.

"It was pure chance brought me up here," Cruz assured the green and scarlet birdman. "When I came popping out of the window of the fair Cleo Waldenbrook's chamber, this seemed a closer refuge than the nearest pedramp six stories below. So I climbed upwards."

"That woman's insatiable." The birdman's beak clicked disapprovingly.

"On the contrary," said Cruz, eyes on the stairwell. "I had the lady completely sated and was about to take my leave when the rev returned home a good hour ahead of time."

"Well, sure, that's because he's on reruns all this month," explained the musician. "Always runs holograph vidtapes of his tedious sermons this time of year. His dippy wife ought to've remembered that simple fact."

"Apparently, in the heat of passion it slipped her peasized mind and so—"

"You may as well come out, you vile fornicator!" boomed Reverend Waldenbrook.

"Is he alluding to me, do you suppose?" Cruz narrowed his left eye and tried to get the outraged cleric lined up in his gunsite.

"Slimy lustridden wretch!"

"Yep," said the birdman with a nod, "he's sure enough addressing you."

"Hell, I'm simply an incurable romantic," explained

the crouching Cruz, "and not the least bit slimy."

"Would that you had heard my sermon this day, you foul fleshly homewrecker! For in it I vilified your very own loathsome type. I said, if I may quote myself, 'Dearly beloved parishioners, although we dwell in a vast city reeking with technological evils and sicklied over with the taint of wickedness, yet we may still . . .' "

"Is this a pretty fair example of his rhetoric?" Cruz asked the bellringer.

His feathery head bobbed. "Sometimes it's duller even."

"Can't figure why there's any call for repeats."

" ' . . . fight off the filthy lustful impulses which seek . . .' "

"Reverend, old chum," called out Cruz, cupping his only hand, "might I suggest a truce?"

"Truce?" bellowed Waldenbrook, thrusting his plump pinkish face again into the open. "There can be no truce, my good man, only swift and sure retribution."

Zzzzzummmmmmm!

Cruz' stungun had hummed.

The beam caught the Most Reverend Waldenbrook smack in the plump forehead. He tottered, wobbled, came stumbling out into the open to drop down, flat out, on the tower floor. His trio of weapons went bouncing and scattering away.

Cruz started to stand. "Wellsir, that didn't prove very difficult."

"Not over yet," warned the birdman.

"Eh?"

"Lord a mercy! Look what the vicious rascal's done to the reverend!"

"Aye, such a foul deed cries out for vengeance!"

Several more loud and angry voices came rolling up out of the stairwell.

"Who might those approaching lads be?"

"His disciples," replied the bird bellringer. "He's got ten or so of them, each and every one large in size and mean and nasty in disposition."

Cruz squatted down once more. "Looks like I'll have to fight on for a spell."

"Not at all necessary," said a Whistler terminal as it materialized just to the left of him.

Terzero is the hottest, steamiest, most jungle-infested of the trio of planets that make up the Trinidad System.

Jack Saint was reflecting on that in his stateroom aboard the lumbering nukepowered riverboat that was carrying him slowly downstream toward one of Terzero's largest port towns. They ought to be docking within the hour.

Despite the aircirc system and two floating fans, the small white cabin was muggy and hot. Saint's bright green skin was dotted with perspiration; his orange hair had lost its springy curl. He was sitting in a lame wicker chair, facing the small table against his cabin's starboard wall.

Perched atop the table was a tri-op portrait, framed in trugold, of the fattest, ugliest, most dimwitted old catwoman on this entire sweaty planet. It was inscribed, in a clumsy scrawl, "To dear, dearest Johan, from his furball, Princess Zorina." Scattered around at the base of the frame of the portrait of the repulsive princess were several realpape business cards that identified Saint as one Johan St. Moritz, General Supervisor of the Trinidad Skymine Development Corp.

Saint ran his tongue over his dry green lips, then rubbed his palms together and strived to rid his mind of thoughts about how far down the ladder of success he'd fallen in the past few months.

"Been having a deuced bad run of luck of late," he muttered. "A frightful waste of potential."

Brow furrowing, bushy orange eyebrows tilting toward each other, Saint began concentrating.

The framed portrait of the catwoman princess quivered and then, with a very faint popping sound, vanished.

Seconds later there was a small thumping sound over on his unmade bunk.

Glancing over his shoulder, the short green man confirmed that the picture had materialized across the cabin.

"Slick as ever," murmured Saint, smiling thinly to himself. "Now then, old man, let us concentrate on the jewel box of the princess."

Just then the door of his stateroom unexpectedly burst open.

"Blackguard!"

"Rogue!"

Narrowing his left eye, Saint scanned the furry couple who'd come barging in on his privacy. "I don't believe we've been introduced," he informed them. "So if you'll kindly withdraw, I—"

"We came aboard at Seton's Landing," said the burly catman in the two-piece checkered travelsuit. He held a kilgun in each piebald paw.

"And poor dear put-upon Aunt Zorina has told us all about you, you fortune hunter," added the husky catwoman on the threshold. She had only one kilgun showing.

"Ah, yes, to be sure." Saint, carefully, rose to his feet. "Then you must be kinsmen of the dear princess."

"I'm Bud Barnstraw and this is my lovely wife Bess," said the checksuited catman as he came stalking in out of the thick, steamy afternoon. "As if you didn't know."

"I assure you, dear fellow, I had not even an inkling of your existence until your surprise entry," said Saint amiably. "Of course, I'm quite flattered at your eagerness to make my acquaintance. Since, however, we'll be docking in but scant minutes, and I'd like very much to change into a fresh suit of—"

"We happen to be her only heirs," Bess Barnstraw informed him, fur bristling.

"She's seventy-nine years old," added Bud.

Bess eased her bulk into the cabin and shut the louvered door. "And you're a nasty fortune hunter."

"We don't intend to let any picklecolored gigolo woo our auntie and have her cut us off without diddly—"

"Sir, I shan't listen to any slurs about my tint." Saint drew himself up to his full five foot three. "I believe one ought to judge a man not by his color, nor by his fur, but by how he—"

"Judging by any standard," interrupted the angry Bud, "you're out to persuade Aunt Zorina to marry you."

"I assure you, old man, that ours is merely a shipboard friendship." Saint glanced casually at his suitcase next to the bunk, the one where his stungun was packed away.

"What we're going to do," explained Bess while digging a paw into her neostraw shoulder bag, "is fix you so you won't romance any more dotty old ladies." From the bag she produced a large folded plyosack.

Saint cleared his throat. "I think, dear people, I'd best make my true intentions clear to you. Crystal clear," he said. "I am not the sort of fellow who weds repulsive old bimbos for their fortunes."

Bud gestured impatiently with one of his guns. "Like heck you aren't."

"I am, trust me, simply a telekinetic cracksman."

"Hm?" Bess blinked, pausing in the unfurling of the big sack.

"I mean, dear lady, that I am but a humble telek." He bowed to her, then to her husband.

Bud's twin kilguns suddenly vanished from his hairy grasp. Seconds later they materialized up near the white ceiling.

Grinning, Saint winked faintly at the perplexed Mrs. Barnstraw.

Her gun disappeared with a faint popping sound. It didn't materialize again.

"Damn it all," said Bud, disappointed. "How the heck are we going to sew you up in this sack, Mr. St. Moritz, and toss you in the river?"

"I rather doubt you are, old boy." Saint opened his green fingers wide and his own stungun materialized in his right hand. Gripping it, he pointed the weapon at the unhappy Barnstraws. "Your interest in the welfare of your dear aunt is most heartwarming. I'll cherish our little meeting."

Zzzzzummmmmmm!

The stunbeam hit Bud first. He gasped, flapped his arms twice and fell to the cabin floor.

Bess said, "Why, you little emerald pipsqueak, where do you get off—"

Zzzzzummmmmmm!

She joined her unconscious husband.

Slipping the gun into his breast pocket, Saint smoothed his jacket. "Ah, how pathetic to see such a great talent as mine thrown away on the likes of these ninnies," he said forlornly. "Bud and Bess . . . gad."

Shrugging, Saint pressed one palm against his green forehead. He concentrated on the jewel case up in the princess' cabin one deck above.

Seconds later it was in his hand.

"Damn, just goes to show what a rotten judge of character I am."

Turning, Saint saw that the door of his cabin was once more open. Framed in the doorway was the captain of the ship, a portly lizardman in a two-piece gold-and-blue unisuit. "Was there something, Captain?" he inquired. "I fear I didn't hear your knock."

"I actually believed you were a man of honor and integrity," said the captain, a sad look touching his scaly brownish face. "In fact, I came barging in here to discuss the buying of a block of Trinidad Skymine Development Corporation stock." He struck his chest with his fist, causing his gold braid to jingle. "Now I find that you are not only a thief, Mr. St. Moritz, but a murderer as well."

"Captain, I had you down as a chap who kept his head," said Saint. "These two are far from being defunct, and I was about to report to you the fact that they'd wandered into my digs and fainted when you—"

"You'll have a chance to refute all the charges I'm going to bring soon as we dock," the captain informed him coldly. "Right now, however, I intend to summon several of my surliest crewmen to haul you to the brig, sir."

"Old man, I've always found incarceration of any sort deuced uncomfortable." Saint lunged at the captain.

He succeeded in tipping the larger man over and, as the captain dropped back onto the yellow deck planks, Saint left his cabin to go running along the deck.

"Help! Escaping killer!" roared the sprawled captain.

Saint hesitated only long enough to thrust the jewel case into the waist of his trousers before sprinting to the rail and, gracefully, vaulting over it.

He hit the tepid river with a whomping splash and

went sinking down in the brown silty water.

Seconds later and several yards from the ship, he resurfaced, about a quarter-mile from the jungly shore.

"For a chap in my tip top condition this swim'll be a piece of cake."

The captain apparently had decided not to halt his craft and give chase, because, when the green man pulled himself up on the mossy stretch of overgrown shore, using the gnarled root of the nearest bluish tree to help him, the ship was already fading away in the hot afternoon haze.

"Excellent, first rate! Couldn't have devised a better test ourselves."

Resting on his heels, Saint brushed his sopping orange hair off his muddy forehead. He frowned over at the computer terminal that floated in the air near the trunk of a squat palm tree.

"One does hope, old thing, you're not a minion of the law."

"I'm Whistler," explained the voxbox of the terminal. "Representing the Whistler Interplanetary Investigation Agency."

Saint shook water off his dripping sleeves. "Come to arrest me, have you?"

"Nope, we want to hire you."

"To do an honest job, do you mean?"

"Exactly."

"Jove," said Saint thoughtfully as he rose, dripping, to his feet, "I may have sunk low enough to take you up on that."

3

It continued to rain on Barnum, a thin misty rain that turned the afternoons a pale, quiet grey.

Jared Smith was looking, and feeling, considerably better than he had three days earlier. "Sure, I feel pretty good," he told the thickset middle-aged scientist the Whistler Agency had assigned to look after him.

"That's discouraging," remarked Doc Winner. "You ought to be feeling at least marvelous by now, if not outright stupendous. The cleverly plotted combination of diet, vitamin injections, dormtherapy and face-to-face bull sessions I've been using on you is guaranteed to—"

"I tend to be a shade pessimistic."

"The shots alone should've wiped that out," fretted Winner as he paced the walled garden they were in.

The rain was kept out by an unseen force screen, one of Doc Winner's inventions.

Smith was sitting in a sewdowicker lawn chair, legs stretched straight out, for his daily interview. "Suppose you fill me in a bit more on the assignment you folks have in mind for me.''

Doc Winner tugged at his greying muttonchop whiskers. ''You know the planet Zegundo very well,'' he said, making another slow circuit of the dry flagstones. ''Know every nook and cranny, for instance, of Selva Territory.''

''I grew up there.''

''Weren't born there, though.''

''Nope, I was born in the next territory over, Sombra.'' Smith rubbed at his chin with his thumb knuckle. ''There was a border war, some of us were relocated. My parents, along with quite a few others, were killed and . . .'' He shrugged. ''About forty of us eventually got sent to Horizon House to live.''

Winner stopped pacing. ''You haven't yet mentioned Doctor Noah Westerland in these little autobiographical interludes, Jared,'' he pointed out. ''Any reason?''

''No. Doctor Westerland ran the place. In fact, it was his home,'' replied Smith. ''He and his wife turned part of the mansion, an enormous joint, over to us refugee kids. Westerland was doing research for the Trinidad Interplanet Government at the time.''

''I know, yes. You liked him?''

Smith nodded.

''And now?''

''He's dead.''

''Apparently so.'' Winner came striding over to seat himself in a white chair facing Smith. ''He died, we are told, seven years ago on Zegundo.''

''You sound like maybe you think he isn't dead.''

Spreading his stubby-fingered hands wide, Doc Winner answered with, ''You were quite fond of his daughter, Jennifer Westerland.''

''In my youth,'' he said. ''Starting about the time I was seventeen.''

"It lasted awhile."

"We had a . . . romance, which continued during the time I was in the Territorial Police." Smith looked up at the rain.

"Her father suggested the romance cease."

"He did." Smith fell silent, frowning.

"They called all of you the Horizon Kids. There was quite a bit of media coverage on you lovable little tykes."

"Yep, there was."

"You keep in touch with any of the kids?"

Smith shook his head. "Not a one."

"There were originally forty-three children in residence during that protracted wartime emergency. Some of them, yourself included, lived at Horizon House for nearly a decade."

"All of this, does it have something to do with the job?"

Winner tugged at a sidewhisker. "You've heard we're nicknamed Suicide, Inc.," he said. "Media twaddle, but it's not bad publicity. Impresses some of our nitwit clients. Actually, however, ninety percent of the jobs we tackle are relatively simple, straightforward assignments with a minimum of risk."

"And the one you have in mind for me is one of these easy, nondangerous ones?"

"Precisely," answered the scientist. "The Whistler Agency has thrived because of the clever ways, a good many of them, I modestly admit, cooked up by me, we go about our business. Our staffs are small, our overhead relatively low. What we do is recruit crews for specific jobs. We seek out people with unique or unusual abilities, match them up with the job at hand and function quite impressively. For your particular . . ." He paused, glanced up, then wiped at his plump cheek. "Drop of rain."

"Got through your screen."

"That's not possible." Doc Winner popped to his feet, scowling. "Unlike most similar systems, mine allows for not one single . . . Holy Hannah! Two more."

"About my job?"

Winner was feeling at the pockets of his smock-like yellow jacket. "What?"

"Now that I'm fast returning to marvelous shape and have decided to accept the job offer," said Smith, "I'm sort of anxious to know what the hell I'm going to be asked to do."

"Oh, it's a simple enough chore." He produced an electric screwdriver from one cluttered side pocket. "In the nature of a scavenger hunt." Shoulders slightly hunched, he approached a flowering shrub. "Control box is hidden under this fragrant bit of foliage. The flowers, and a snappy shade of purple they are indeed, bloom the whole year round. Thing also repels all major insects. My idea."

"The flowers smell somewhat like old boots." Smith had joined him near the high garden wall.

"Do you think so? Well, I was trying for something offbeat, not being fond of sweet cloying scents myself."

"What am I going to be hunting for, Doc?"

Dropping to his knees, Winner began poking around at the roots of the plant. "People, my boy, you'll be rounding up people. In fact, your old school chums. Former residents of Horizon House," he said. "Ah, here's the dang control box, under this glob of super-efficient synthetic fertilizer I inven—"

"Are these people missing or—"

"Missing, or lost. Five of 'em." Winner pried the lid off the small gunmetal box that sat on the loamy soil. "Assumption is that most of 'em are still on Zegundo, but scattered to the winds."

"Who wants them?"

"Our client."

"Who is?"

"Well, no wonder this was on the fritz, no wonder. This unappealing blue bug has snuck inside my box and committed suicide in the midst of my ingenious and colorful circuitry. Shoo." With thumb and forefinger Doc Winner lifted the tiny blue corpse free of the box. "A Trinidad-based company called Triplan, Ltd. is financing your mission. Even as we speak, which Whistler may've mentioned, we're merrily scouring the planets in search of a crackajack crew for you."

Walking back to his chair, Smith sat. "Would your contact at Triplan be a guy named Benton Arloff?"

Winner shut the box, nudged it into its former position, and grunted to his feet. "Arloff's the lad who married Jennifer Westerland a couple years back, I believe," he said. "Yes, he's our client, Jared. Do you object to working for him and his firm?"

After a few silent seconds Smith answered, "Nope. But why's Arloff so anxious to find these missing Horizon Kids?"

"A sentimental gesture," said Doc Winner. "What he, along with his dear wife and her sweet greyhaired mother, has in mind is a reunion of all you tots. Years have passed, you're all full grown, time to get together once again to wax tearful about old times."

Smith, slouched in his chair, watched him for a while, a thin grin on his tanned face. "You really believe, Doc, that that's their only motive?"

"Not a bit," he admitted. "You ought to have fun finding out what they're really up to."

A long drop of rain came falling down through the force screen to splash on his broad, flat nose.

4 ═══════════════════════

Smith turned his back on the vast enormity of space, left the view window and crossed the spaceliner saloon to one of the several empty tables.

At the small floating table next to his sat a large greenish lizardman, slightly slumped and sniffing into a polkadot plyochief. After wiping at his weepy eyes, he gazed over at Smith. "You have a kindly, understanding face, sir," he said in a croaky voice.

Smith brought up a hand and touched his face. "I do?"

The five empty mulled skullpop mugs on the lizard's tabletop hopped when he released a heartfelt sigh. "I judge you to be the sort of man upon whom I can unburden myself."

"That's an error in judgment, because—"

"Permit me to introduce myself." He was poking and probing his scaly hands into the pockets of his two-piece checkered travelsuit. "I think I must've blown my nose on the last business card I had. At any rate, I am Norman Vincent Bagdad."

"Mr. Bagdad, I truly don't want to hear your—"

"I am a practicing polygamist."

"That's of no—"

"I have four wives." He held up a quartet of green fingers. "Four. And where are they now?"

"Fooling around?"

The lizardman gave a sad shake of his head. "Would that they were," he said. "No, they're in our luxurious cabin, rehearsing."

"Rehearsing what?" Smith noticed that the servobot was three tables off.

"Their act. My wives are the Sophisticates." He studied Smith's face for a sign of recognition.

"Never heard of them. What do they do?"

Bagdad laughed hollowly. "By George, sir, this is refreshing," he said. "I'm glad we began this pleasant discourse, because it gives me a fresh perspective on my—"

"It's really not a discourse, Bagdad. I'd prefer to sit in solitude and contemp—"

"The Sophisticates, sir, happen to be the hottest singing group in the Hellquad System of planets," the lizard explained. "They're enroute now to the Trinidads for a series of SRO concerts. Their last musivid album just went lead."

"That's good?"

"On the Hellquads, where there's very little metal, it's akin to going platinum."

"Oh, so?"

The big lizardman said, "Try to imagine how you'd feel, sir, if every single one of your wives started straying from your hearth and home in order to pursue a show business career." He leaned closer. "You've really never seen their hit single *Don't Sit Under the Utumbo Tree With—*"

"Okay, what'll she be, cobber?" The tall, wide copperplated servobot had rolled over to Smith's table. He stood grinning, silver teeth sparkling in his ball of a head. "Name's Think-A-Drink." Holding up his right hand, he revealed that all five fingers were spiggots. "You name it, I'll pour it, buddy."

Smith said, "Sparkling water."

Think-A-Drink's metallic eyelids fluttered; his round coppery head did a complete turn. "Do these old earflaps deceive me? A big strapping lad like you asking for . . . ugh . . . a pansy drink like bubble water?"

Smith grinned thinly. "Sparkling water."

The big robot whapped his broad metal chest. "That's no challenge, bucko," he said. "I mean to say, I can mix thousands of drinks and potations, the favorite concoctions of the four corners of the blinking universe, do you see. From an Earth Martini to a Venusian Sidney K. Brainslammer. I can whip up a Pink Snerg, a Spacewalloper's Lament, a—"

"Sparkling water," said Smith. "No ice."

Think-A-Drink bestowed a coppery sneer upon him. "Coming up, Percy." Opening a panel in his side, he extracted a chilled plazglass. Then, the sneer still resting on his metallic lips, he pointed his little finger at the glass. A thin stream of club soda gushed out. "One sparkling water."

"Thanks."

Think-A-Drink rattled to the table on the other side of Smith. "What'll she be, cobber?" he asked of the small, greyhaired man who sat with his back to Smith.

"As I was saying," resumed Norman Vincent Bagdad. "I've always been a man who dotes on routine. When you have four wives, why then you can schedule your romantic life in such a—"

"Cheers." Smith lifted his glass, took a sip. Frowning suddenly, he turned to watch the robot pouring the drink for the man at the next table.

"Something wrong, sir?" inquired the lizardman.

Smith sniffed the air. "Damn," he said, getting quickly up and free of his chair.

He lunged, swung at the plazglass in the greyhaired man's hand and knocked it from his grasp.

The glass went spinning, splashing sticky green liquid on both of them. It hit the tabletop, bounced twice, and plunged to the black-carpeted saloon floor.

"I think your drink was poisoned," said Smith, wiping his hand on his trouser leg.

"I know damn well it was, Smith," said the sourfaced little man. "And you've just advertised the fact to half the lamebrains who're traveling on this tub."

"Frosting," muttered Smith as he waded along the corridor leading to his cabin.

The ribbed plaz floor was awash with nearly a foot of lukewarm sudsy water.

"Is that, you know, some Barnum curse word that the boys exchange around the locker room?" A slim, pretty blonde young woman had emerged from a sliding-paneled doorway just to his right. She wore a snug-fitting space steward unisuit of green and gold.

"Actually, no, Mercy Jane," said Smith, halting in the tepid foamy water.

"I like to keep up on as much jargon as I can. So, you know, if people are exclaiming, 'Oh, frosting!' in moments of stress, why I want—"

"I was commenting to myself that the corridor being all futzed up was just so much frosting on the cake. The cake being a frumus that just took place up in the saloon."

"I get it. Simile and metaphor," she said, smiling brightly.

"More or less."

"The laundrybots are having some problems," explained the pretty spaceflight attendant. "Like, you know, they started falling down a lot. That oftentimes happens, but don't tell anybody I told you. Usually right after we make our hyperspace jump, which we just did moments ago. Me, I get sort of woozy in the tummy, but the laundrybots fall over and lots of water gets spilled."

"About how long do you think it'll be before the water gets cleaned up?"

"Depends, you know, on how soon the vacuubots wake up."

"This is their nap period?"

She laughed. "No, it's simply that, you know, they pass out every darn time we make a hyperspace jump," she said. "I hope all this isn't giving you a bad impression of the SS Pearl of the Universe."

"Your kind attentions, Mercy Jane, have more than made up for any little inconvenience like soggy ankles." Grinning at her, he resumed his walk along the damp corridor.

"Would it cheer you up any if we, you know, went to your bunk and fooled around?" she asked, sloshing along beside him. "I have the next twenty-two minutes free."

"It usually takes me that long just to get undressed," Smith told her. "Besides, I'm expecting a visitor. I appreciate the offer, though."

"You don't find me repulsive, do you?"

"Not at all."

"With so many different types of life in the universe, you know, a girl can't always tell who she appeals to and who she doesn't. Or should that be whom?" Mercy Jane said. "We even have a passenger on this very flight who's traveling with four lizardladies. *Four*. Urf, that makes my skin all crawly."

Halting at his door, Smith pressed his hand to the printrec plate. The door stuttered open. "Thanks for the kind thoughts."

"Think nothing of it." She patted his backside and hurried away.

Smith entered his cabin, pleased to notice that the floor was dry.

"Thought for a moment you were going to drag that skinny lass in here," said Whistler, as he materialized near the bunk.

"So did I." Smith dropped into a floating plaz slingchair." "Then I decided, duty first."

"I've got some new info for you," said the detective agency terminal.

"First," suggested Smith, "let me give you some."

5 ═══════════════════

"So tell me what . . . oops!" Whistler's screen turned all at once an intense crimson.

"You okay?"

"Hush." The terminal swooped down near the floor.

From its underside came a thin line of green light. The pulsating beam cut a small oval swatch out of the thermocarpet.

A tiny flat spybug had been nesting under the rug.

Whistler sucked it up into its interior.

Smith said, "Who the hell planted—"

"Silence." The terminal floated up to the sewdometal ceiling.

From within one of the three floating light balls Whistler extracted a second bugging device, this one larger.

"Now?" asked Smith, settling back into his chair.

"That's the lot." Whistler drifted down to a spot some four feet above the floor. "All those months of booze must've addled your wits, Smitty. You should've spotted these eavesdropping gadgets.''

"My fault, sure," admitted Smith. "Thing is, you guys assured me this assignment was simple and routine. That lulled me into—"

"Being lulled is one thing, being jackass stupid is another."

"Speaking of stupidity, how come you guys didn't mention that the Trinidad Law Bureau was interested in this case? If you did know and forgot to tell me, that was stupid, too."

"What makes you think TLB's involved?"

Smith grinned. "I just bumped into Deac Constiner up in the saloon."

"Constiner? He's just about their best man. Are you certain he—"

"He didn't give me a signed deposition, no," said Smith. "He claims he's just going back home after attending a law conference on Barnum."

"That might be true."

"Might, but I think he got wind of us somehow and got himself down to Barnum so he could catch the *SS Pearl of the Universe* and keep an eye on me."

Whistler produced a faint buzzing sound. "Your hunch may just be right Smitty," it said. "The under-the-rug snooping device tests out as standard Trinidad Law Bureau equipment."

"Then they are interested in me," Smith said. "That's odd, if all that's involved is a class reunion."

"Isn't it, though?" Whistler commenced humming again. "Tell you something else of interest, chum. The second spy gadget my keen senses detected is of maverick design."

"Not TLB?"

"Nothing they've ever utilized before. I can't even ID

it right off," replied the floating terminal. "It ain't of Trinidad or Barnum System manufacture."

Smith held out his hand, palm up. "Let me see."

"Listen, inside me is equipment clever enough to identify, eventually, just about any—"

"A look."

"Okay." The bug dropped from beneath the terminal, went drifting over to Smith. "But if my highly—"

"Earth." Smith tossed the little device up and caught it after examining it.

"The planet Earth in the Earth System?"

"That Earth, yep."

"Heck of a ways from here. I can't see why Earth agents'd be at all interested in—"

"The equipment comes from Earth," said Smith. "But I've seen people out here use stuff like this."

"This seems to indicate there's more than one agent interested in you."

"It does." Smith eyed the terminal. "Have you guys told me everything?"

"So help me, cross my heart."

"I'll have to nose around the liner more than I—"

"Don't go getting bumped off like . . . um . . ."

Smith stood. "Bumped off like who?"

"Oh, that was just a figure of—"

"Who got killed on this case already, Whistler?"

The screen blushed pink for an instant. "Well, it wasn't one of our operatives," it said in a subdued tone. "An agent working in our client's Security Division died under suspicious circumstances while trying to find some of the missing Horizon Kids. That's one reason why Triplan decided to come to us and not—"

"Suspicious how?"

"Oh, his skycar exploded. Scattered him all over a

stretch of Zegundo woodlands. They never found enough pieces of the man or his skycar to be absolutely sure if it was an accident or a rubout.''

"Simple case, no danger." Smith sat, slouched. "This ties in with the attempt on Constiner, too, probably."

"I'm not aware of any—"

"Just happened." Smith pointed a thumb at the ceiling. "Up in the saloon. Someone tampered with the servobot so that it introduced a fairly obscure but deadly herbal poison into Constiner's drink. The stuff has a very faint scent and I noticed it."

"What did you do?"

"Knocked the damn glass out of his hand before he drank it."

"Was that wise?"

"I didn't know it was Constiner until after I acted," said Smith. "Bastard wasn't all that grateful, claiming he'd spotted the stuff, too, but was going to pretend to kick off. Then see who came nosing around his mortal remains."

"That's not a bad plan, much better than your—"

"I'm a shade rusty, I admit. Don't worry, I won't keep making mistakes."

"Any notion who rigged the 'bot?"

"I managed to watch while Constiner dismantled the robot back in the pantry. Not a trace of who did the fiddling."

"Most likely the same agent who decorated your quarters with this unorthodox snooping device."

"Possibly."

"Stands to reason, Smitty, because—"

"You guys don't know everything yet," Smith pointed out. "It could be there are a dozen different agents, each one with a different boss, interested in this mess. And every one of them may have orders to do me in next."

"Why not try to thrive on the challenge. The added danger should buoy you up, make—"

"I don't especially want to die," explained Smith.

"You won't," Whistler assured him. "Your record shows you have an almost supernatural knack for survival."

"Up to now."

"This negative attitude is what led you to end up in the gutter, Smitty," said the terminal. "You have to look on the bright—"

"Let's move on to the subject of my crew," he suggested. "You were supposed to drop in here to tell me who you've hired."

"If you hadn't sidetracked me with all this Gloomy Gus chitchat I'd have long since—"

"Fill me in."

Whistler floated back a few feet farther away from him. "Before I fill you in on the excellent team we've put together," he said, "I want you to make a little vow."

"Vow?"

"That you won't swear and yell and berate me in case . . . I merely say *in case* you notice . . . in case they don't meet with your complete approval."

"What sort of dimwitted louts have you saddled me—"

"Hear me out with a minimum of complaining and cursing, please. This is, after all, something of a rush situation and—"

"Okay, okay," said Smith. "I won't bitch and moan. It's a promise. Go on."

He was very nearly able to keep his promise.

6

Someone whacked on the door of Smith's cabin, hard, several times.

He eased up out of his chair, touched the door switch. The door coughed, jiggled, slid open.

Deac Constiner stood on the threshold. "Your frapping corridor's full of sand."

"Two hours ago it was soapy water."

The Trinidad Law Bureau agent's frown deepened. "I was a little harsh with you in the saloon," he said. "Implied you were a bigger halfwit than you probably are."

"Come on in," invited Smith. "An apology from you is an event."

Shaking yellow sand off his neohyde boots, the small lawman entered. "What'd you do with the damn bug I had planted in here?"

While they both glanced down at the small circular hole in the carpeting, Smith replied, "Got rid of it."

"Do you realize those things cost five hundred trubux apiece?"

"When we get to Zegundo, I'll show you a place you can buy them for two hundred."

Constiner sat, uninvited, on the edge of the bunk. "Did you find any other bugs in here?"

"Should I have?"

"Let's put our cards on the table," said Constiner. "We're both interested in the same case. See? I'm being frank with you."

"After you realized I was on to you."

The lawman said, "You used to be a pretty fair operative. At least you weren't as much of a stumble-bum as most of the lunks in the Territorial cops. I know you went blooey over a dame, but hell, that can happen to any of us."

"Not to you."

"I'm an exception," admitted Constiner.

"What exactly," inquired Smith, settling into a chair, "is this case we're both working on?"

Constiner gave a dry chuckle. "You tell me, Smith."

"I'm looking for some people."

"Me, too."

"Why?"

"Same reason you are."

"To get them," asked Smith, "to attend the Horizon Kids' reunion?"

New lines joined the large selection on Constiner's leathery forehead. "Is that really what you think you're doing?"

"It is what I'm doing."

"Here I just get through telling you that maybe you're not a dimwit and you act like a dimwit," the TLB man complained. "Use your damn noggin. Who ran Horizon House?"

"Westerland."

"And what was he the head of? The freewheeling government research agency known as the Miracle Office."

"Then all this maybe has something to do with an invention of his?"

Constiner folded his hands over his knee. "What do you think?"

"Is Westerland really dead?"

"Sure, he's dead. You know that as well as . . . hold it. Do you have information to the contrary?"

Smith grinned. "Nope."

"They never found his body after that nukeboat explosion," said Constiner.

Smith asked, "Who else is interested in this?"

"Could be most anybody."

"Can you narrow that some?"

"No."

"Who tried to poison you?"

"Could be most anybody."

Smith nodded. "I appreciate your taking me into your confidence this way, Deac," he said. "I learn all sorts of stuff."

Leaving the bunk, Constiner said, "We'll be arriving on Zegundo in a few minutes. No doubt I'll be running into you again."

"No doubt," agreed Smith.

7

Smith didn't feel as though he'd come home. Walking along the stretch of orange beach that fronted the cottage the Whistler Agency had rented for him, he didn't feel this was a homecoming. He was back on the planet Zegundo, back in Selva Territory, yet he didn't feel much of anything.

"Correction," he said aloud, looking out across the clear blue of the sea.

When he thought about Jennifer Westerland and the fact that she was probably in the territory's capital city right now, not more than forty miles from him, he did feel as . . . hell, that had nothing to to do with the business at hand.

Far out in the hazy morning a scatter of bright yellow birds were gliding low over the quiet water.

"And her name's Jennifer Arloff now," he reminded himself. "Has been for—"

An incredible grating noise started up behind him.

Spinning, drawing the stungun he wore openly in his belt holster, Smith found himself facing the childsized servobot who came with the cottage. "The music, Bosco." Smith let his gun slide back to rest.

"How's that, tuan?" The silvery little robot cupped his metal hand to his plaz-trimmed earhole.

Smith reached out, tapped the portable radiobox that was magnetically attached to the mechanism's tank-shaped torso and was blaring out some kind of godawful sound that might just be music. "Turn it off."

"Ah, forgive me, bwana." Bosco bowed, took a back-step, clicked off the radio. "It is merely that I've been designed to be not only efficient, loyal and trust-worthy but also hep."

"Hep?"

"I dig the jive, sahib," amplified Bosco. "I'm a killerdiller."

Something occurred to Smith. "Could that cater-wauling have been a group called the Sophisticates?"

"You're pretty hep yourself, gate. It was indeed, the solid goods," replied Bosco. "Their latest hit platter, entitled *He's A Boogie Woogie Lycanthrope From*—"

"Tell me the true purpose of your visit."

"Ah, enough pop culture chitchat, yes. You are perfectly right to remind me of my mission, marse," said the pintsized robot. "We're being encroached on, I fear."

"Explain," requested Smith, gazing up at the glaz, plaz and neowood beach cottage a hundred yards away.

"A large, one might almost dub it flashy, landcar has rolled up in front of our domicile, sire," he said. "Two relatively unsavory gentlemen are disembarking and before I give them the customary bum's rush, I thought I'd best consult with you as to—"

"One is a big dark guy with a sleazy moustache, looks like he's suffering from terminal horniness?" asked Smith. "The other's a diminutive green gent you wouldn't trust even with your everyday silverware?"

Bosco's little metal hands made a bonging sound when he clapped them together in appreciation. "You are most astute and hep, tuan," he exclaimed. "For you have deduced exactly what these two squatters look like without even—"

"I'm afraid," cut in Smith as he started for the cottage, "they're the guests I've been expecting."

"Ah, sad," said Bosco. "That's a pisser, bwana."

The morning sunlight came slanting into the parlor and caused Cruz' right arm to glisten. It was an impressive arm, made of stainless impervium and packed with gadgets and weaponry. With his real left hand the large dark man was stroking his handsome black moustache and watching Smith from his wicker sling-chair. "Does self-pity come under new business or old?" Cruz inquired.

Smith was slouched alone on the tin sofa. "Do I look that glum?"

"We're none of us," put in the green-complected Jack Saint, "in tophole form, old boy, or we wouldn't be employed by the Whistler blokes."

"You're running this operation and I get the impression you might want a somewhat less disreputable crew," Cruz said to Smith. "If so, air your feelings. Next Saint and I can do some wailing, complaining about harsh fate and the like, and then we'll get down to business."

Smith grinned. "When I first heard who the Whistler folks had stuck me with," he admitted, "I was nonplussed. No, make that ticked off. But then . . . well, I read over your dossiers a few more times and—"

"One hopes they're not still using that beastly photograph of me taken when I wore my hair parted in the middle." Saint bounced once in his glazbottom rocker.

"They are," said Smith. "Anyway, I decided that both of you are well qualified for this job. Cruz, you know the wilds of this planet, and you're a first-rate tracker and guide. You do tend to—"

"I get distracted," admitted Cruz. "Pretty ladies are as lodestones, deflecting me from the path to true virtue." He shrugged. "I'm going to make a supreme effort to reform, at least for the duration of this excursion."

"Saint, you're an excellent telek."

"I'm a corker," he acknowledged, rubbing his green palms together.

Smith opened the pale blue folder that rested on the plaz coffee table in front of him. "Myself, I haven't been in such terrific shape for the past year or so," he said. "I'd like to assure you that I've reformed, but I can't guarantee it. We'll all just have to put up with each other and hope for the best."

Cruz tugged at the tip of his moustache with his metal fingers. "Once I courted and wooed a substantially structured lady whose husband was vice president of a banking satellite orbiting Murdstone's second moon," he said, glancing over at the oval stained glass window nearest him. "She thought that openly talking about money was just about the filthiest thing you could do. Often were the times I excited her by whispering, 'One thousand trubux down,' and 'Seventy five trubux an hour,' in her pudgy pink ear. The point of this amorous recollection is that I have never shared that view.

Whistler offered me ten thousand trubux for this, half in front. How about you gents?"

"The same, old man."

"I'm getting twenty thousand," Smith told them.

"Since you're the boss," decided Cruz, "that's okay."

Resting an elbow on the rocker arm, Saint leaned toward him. "I acquired an impressive ruby necklace from a plumpish banker's wife on Murdstone some three years since," he confided. "Might it be, do you think, the same lady?"

"This lady's name was—"

"Let's commence," cut in Smith, picking up a sheet of faxpape from the open folder. "The agency's already given you a general idea of what we're supposed to accomplish."

"Find a bunch of strayed tots," said Saint. "Sounds deuced simple, I must say."

"What they may not've told you is that at least one of our client's own security people has been killed while working on this simple task."

Saint sat up, his rocker wiggling. "One doesn't expect class reunions to be fraught with such violence."

"This is more than a reunion," said Smith. "Now, maybe the Whistler Agency doesn't know much more than they told us, and maybe they do. What I know is that the Trinidad Law Bureau, which is the interplanetary police force for all three of the planets in this system, has a man working on this same job."

Cruz asked, "Who?"

"Deac Constiner."

"Heartless bloke," murmured Saint.

"He's good, though," said Cruz. "TLB doesn't stick ops like him on a simple job."

"There's also somebody else interested in me, in Constiner and probably in the missing Horizon Kids," said Smith. He filled them in on what had happened aboard the spaceliner.

"We ought to ask for extra hazard pay," suggested Cruz, when he'd finished.

"There'll be a bonus if we bring this off."

Saint said, "Why is everyone so dashed interested in these particular kiddies?"

"Horizon House was the home of Doctor Noah Westerland," answered Smith. "He ran a research facility for the triplanet government. Most people called it the Miracle Office."

"Ah, good old MO," said Saint, scratching at his curly red hair. "They're the jolly chaps who invented the dustgun, the braintap machine, Kilgas #3 and sundry other droll weapons and knickknacks."

"Doctor Westerland is deceased," said Cruz. "But it's possible these missing Horizon House alums are privy to one of his dark secrets, huh?"

"That's sure as hell the impression I get from Constiner."

Cruz sucked in his cheek. "Therefore, comrades, our mission becomes a shade more challenging," he said. "We have to find the lost HH gang *and* we ought to learn why they're really wanted."

"I'd like to begin this way," said Smith. "Saint, with your telek abilities and your knack for ingratiating yourself into people's confidence—"

"It's plain and simple charm, old man, not a knack," corrected the compact green man. "Can't help it, don't you know, I am just naturally appealing to one and all."

"Use your charm to get a look at the Triplan, Ltd. files relating to this business," Smith told him.

"They're our clients and I'm assuming they must know the real reason for this hunt."

"Headquarters near here, I do believe, in the territorial capital?"

"Yep." Smith turned to Cruz. "I've got a list of the five missing people. I knew them all, so—"

"That's right, you're also a grad of that establishment."

"I am, yeah. Point is, I've gone over the field reports of the Triplan security people." He picked up a sheaf of yellow faxpape. "In at least one case I think they missed following up a lead, simply because they didn't know as much as I do about these five. Cruz and I will start tracking while Saint—"

"Begging your pardon, gate." Bosco came toddling into the bright parlor. "I hate to crash your jam session, cats, yet there is an important call on the pixphone for the sahib."

Smith asked, "Who?"

"From Triplan, Ltd., tuan," explained the little servobot. "The lady must speak with you at once."

"Lady?"

"Her name is Jennifer Arloff and she mentioned that she is an old friend of yours."

8

She held out her hand, smiling quietly. "I lied to your robot," Jennifer said. "I wasn't calling from Triplan. And I lied to you, too, Jared. This isn't an official client and agency meeting."

Smith shook her hand. "Maybe it isn't a good idea to—"

"But this is about the case. Can we walk for a while?"

He'd come to one of the marinas in the capital to meet her, a long curving stretch of low glaz and neo-wood buildings along the edge of the sea. There was a restaurant nearby where they had met fairly often. A long time ago.

"We can walk," he said.

A faint midday breeze was drifting in across the bright ocean.

"You look," she said, "fit and well."

"You look sad."

"Imagination."

"Probably."

"You're all right, happy and all?"

"Laughing from dawn to dusk."

"There are still times when I miss you, Jared."

"Not too many."

She said, "If you meet my husband, don't mention I called you or talked to you like this."

"Whistler operatives are discreet."

She slowed. "When I learned you'd be working on this, I wanted you to be told everything. My husband didn't agree."

"But you're telling me now anyway."

"Something's happened."

"I know about your security man's being killed."

Jennifer shook her head impatiently. "You remember Hal Larzon?"

"One of the Horizon Kids, sure."

"He's dead." She stopped walking, paused on the white gravel path and looked out at the glittering sea. "He was murdered."

"When?"

"Late yesterday. We found out this morning," she answered. "Whoever did it used a kilgun on him."

"Where was Larzon?"

"Here, in the capital. We'd brought him in for the . . . for the reunion."

Smith said, "His name isn't on my list. Does he tie in in some way with the others?"

"Oh, hell," she said quietly. "The damn reunion is just a cover. Of the forty-three Horizon Kids we're only interested in ten. Half we were able to find on our own, but the others have simply dropped from sight. After Schuster, our security agent, was killed, my husband decided we needed some outside help." Slim shoulders slightly hunched, Jennifer began walking again.

He walked close beside her, careful not to touch her.

"Larzon was one of the ten?"

"Yes, and they got to him."

"Who?"

"We're not sure, but it seems likely that Syndek Industries is involved somehow."

"That's Triplan's largest rival hereabouts."

"Yes, they are."

"Is that how you folks do your business, by killing each other off?"

"You ought to know what it's like on this planet, since you were a lawman here once."

Smith asked, "Why are these ten HH kids on your list?"

"It has to do with . . . with something my father was working on just before he died. I . . . well, I can't give you all the details, but it's important."

"A weapon?"

"No, but something important, and valuable."

"Why wait all this time after your father's death to go tracking people down?"

"We didn't find out about it until . . . until recently."

He watched five small multicolor nukepower boats go gliding along the horizon. "All ten people know the secret?"

"Each knows only a part."

"Ah, a human jigsaw." Smith grinned. "Why'd your dad hide his secret this particular way?"

"It was something . . ." She looked up at him. "He came up with something while he was working for the damn Miracle Office, something he simply didn't want them to have. So he broke his notes and schematics up this way and then destroyed them. His intention was to retrieve all ten parts after he left the government's employ."

"Do the carriers know?"

She lowered her head, kicking at the pale orange sand

at the path's edge. "No. Dad . . . well, he implanted the information by way of electrohypnosis. Each of them is walking around with a part of . . . of the puzzle. When each hears a special trigger word he or she'll go into a trance and recite the buried information or draw a part of the plans."

"Very clever man, your pop. Kindly, good with children and—"

"He was brilliant," she said, angry. "You never liked him, which is why you—"

"You're wrong. I liked him, I was even dumb enough to think of him as a substitute father," Smith told her. "That's why, when he told you to drop me out of your life, I was . . . surprised."

"It wasn't his fault that . . . oh, hell, never mind." She took hold of his arm. "I want you to know what you're really up against, Jared. You're going to have to be careful and—"

"I'm almost always careful."

"I don't want you to be killed . . . or even hurt."

"That's heartwarming."

Jennifer let go of his arm. "You're still a shit at heart, aren't you?" she said, stepping back from him. "Never let anyone do you a favor without treating them like—"

"About Larzon. Did you get the information he had?"

"Yes. We did."

"What about the opposition, Syndek or whoever it might be?"

"There's evidence that some brainprobing was done before he was killed."

"How the hell did your rivals hear about this in the first place?"

"A leak, obviously," she replied, "but we haven't found it yet."

"Okay, what I have to do is find the lost five first

off," he said, "and see that they remain alive and well."

"And watch out for competition."

"Can you give me a list of the whole ten?"

"You don't need to know the—"

"The better informed I am, the safer I feel."

"I'll write the names out for you, but you can't go near any of those we've already—"

"Trust me not to be dumb."

Jennifer stopped walking once again. "Do you realize, Jared, that all the time we've been talking, you've never once used my name?"

"Sorry," he said. "I didn't mean anything by it, Mrs. Arloff."

9

It was Cruz' turn to drive.

Whistling, his tongue pressed against his upper teeth, the big dark man leaned back in the driveseat of their landvan and guided it across the hazy midmorning desert with his real hand on the steering rod.

Smith, slouched in the seat next to him, was watching a well-groomed catman newscaster on the small dash-mounted vidscreen.

The catman was explaining the political situation and military skirmishing that was going on in the Canal Zone of Zegundo. " . . . Control of the Grand Canal has fallen into the hands of the Mizayen Commandos, according to their spokesman Ulu Vak. However, the Qatzir Militiamen dispute this, insisting they still are in possession of the key locks. Their interim leader, Nura Nal, issued a statement to that effect at a press conference held this morning at the Houd Istihmam Yacht Club just before it was blown up. Spokesmen for

Tasmia Malor contest this, maintaining that Malor is still the spiritual leader of the militia and that the canal is controlled by his Qatfia Guards. More on that after this word from Grandma's Candied Bugs. . . ."

"I haven't been in this part of the country for a spell," said Cruz. "Sounds like we still have lots of unrest to contend with."

"The capital, where we're heading, has been quiet lately."

"I have," admitted Cruz, "a real disinclination to get knocked off as an innocent bystander in somebody else's fracas."

Smith grinned. "That's not likely."

"This lad we're searching for, Oscar Ruiz. You really figure he's hereabouts?"

"The Triplan security guy trailed him as far as the Canal Zone Capital. He worked for near a year as a Freefall Poker dealer at one of the canaledge casinos. Then, about three weeks ago, he dropped from sight."

"Gamblers are like that, footloose and restless."

"This isn't in Ruiz' dossier, but he used to talk to me about wanting to visit a place called the Shrine," said Smith. "It's a religious setup and—"

"Thousands of dedicated pilgrims wend their way there every year."

"Right, and the Shrine's only twenty miles south of the capital, out in the Red Desert. Seems likely to me that Ruiz, once he had some money again, decided to make his pilgrimage at last."

Cruz smoothed his moustache with his metal thumb. "Must be deeply satisfying to have faith in some . . . oops!"

The nukemotor made an odd noise.

Chunkachug!

Then a series of them.

Chugabank! Wamgonk! Kaplow!

Their landvan shimmied, hopped twice, ceased moving.

"Trouble." Smith opened his door.

"Doesn't sound too serious." Cruz eased out onto the desert roadway.

The heat came swooping down on both men, prickly and steamy.

Smith popped the engine lid. "You're supposed to be an expert on mechanics."

Nodding, Cruz pushed a button on his wrist. His forefinger pinged open at the tip, releasing a small screwdriver blade. "It's just the rimfire gudgeons that came loose. A little tightening is all we need."

"Design that arm yourself?" Smith glanced up, watching the half-dozen crimson buzzards circling them high up.

"I had a bit of assistance. Once out on Peregrine I wooed a titian-tressed lady whose second husband . . . they wed them in pairs in that particular locale . . . her number two hubby was a veritable electronics whiz and 'twas he who—"

"New spot of trouble approaching over yonder," Smith interrupted to point out.

A small cloud of reddish dust had appeared to the right of them, about a mile off and coming ever closer.

"Might be commandos, militiamen, guards, guerillas or mercenaries." Cruz ceased laboring on the engine and pushed another spot on his metal wrist. A small telescope popped out of the end of his thumb. "None of the above." He offered Smith a look.

There were five mounted men rapidly approaching them on groutback. Big, green snakemen clad in flowing safron-and-gold robes. "Slavers," recognized Smith.

"Same conclusion I reached." Retracting the spyglass, he shut the engine lid. "We ought to be able to handle five."

Nodding, Smith trotted around the landvan and opened the rear door. From within he took two stunrifles. "Let's try to palaver first."

"I don't need one of those. I'll rely on my trusty arm."

"Don't kill anybody unless—"

"I know the Whistler Agency code of ethics, never fear. Fact is, it matches that of the Cruzes. For untold generations no Cruz has . . ." His voice trailed off as the slavers reined up some two hundred yards away.

One of the snakemen left the group, urging his sturdy sixlegged mount toward the landvan.

"Hail, scum," he called out in his raspy voice.

"He's not getting off to a very cordial start." Cruz rubbed his real fingers along his glistening metal arm.

Smith narrowed his eyes. "Is that you, Rudy?"

The snakeman chuckled. "Glorioski! It can't be Smitty?" He came galloping right up to him, dropped free of his ornate saddle. "Talk about a small darn universe. I heard you'd gone to pieces . . . broken heart, was it? . . . and had become a pathetic stewbum off on some hick planet." Hands on hips, he surveyed Smith. "But, heck, you don't look all that terrible."

"I'm on the road to recovery." He lowered his rifle. "What happened to your miniature golf course in the capital?"

"Aw, I overextended myself, for one thing," the robed slaver admitted. "When I added the Venusianfried poutfish franchise, that was the shagarat that busted the snerg's back. And the fact, which the son of a gun I bought the golf course from forgot to tell me, that the neighborhood gorilla men liked to stage their tribal dances on the fourteenth hole. You ever try to play through a couple dozen gorilla men giving out with the victory cry of the bull ape?''

"I had that experience once out on Murdstone," put in Cruz. " 'Twas while I was pursuing the blonde and marginally virginal youngest daughter of an archeology prof who specialized in defiling ancient tombs and—''

"Rudy, this is Cruz."

The snakeman held out a green scaly hand. "Any friend of Smitty's.''

"I'm here on business," explained Smith while the two shook hands. "You and your cronies weren't planning to attack us?''

"Heck, no," said Rudy. "You can just go on your merry way. And, say, if you get anywhere near my old place, look up the new owner. Mention my name and he'll fix the both of you up with poutfish dinners. But don't go, a word to the wise, on any night there's a double full moon. Gorilla nights.''

"Appreciate the thought.''

"Listen, it was darn nice seeing you again." The big snakeman, bright robes flapping, swung back up onto his grout. "Pleasure meeting you, too, Cruz." He turned his mount, waved at them and rode off to rejoin his associates.

"Fix the engine," said Smith quietly, "fast.''

"Is Rudy likely to go back on his word?''

"Nope, but Rudy's never been able to keep in charge of anything for very long.''

"I'll hasten," promised Cruz.

•   •   •

The catman's crimson turban rose straight up off his furry orange head, unraveling in the process.

"Begone," suggested Cruz, lowering his metal hand.

"Ah, effendi," the catman attempted to explain as the unfurled turban settled back down, festooning his head and shoulders, "I merely brushed against you on this foul and crowded thoroughfare. I am not a dip nor a member of the lightfingered gentry. Nay, rather I—"

"Depart," advised Cruz, "or I'll use my built-in shockrod yet again, chum."

"As you suggest." Bowing, smoothing down his on-edge fur, the man went stumbling away through the afternoon crowd.

"Where were we in our lively conversation?" Cruz asked Smith.

"You were about to intrude in my private affairs."

The street was paved with cobblestones of a faded gold color; it was narrow and twisting. Striped awnings hung out over many of the sandcolored buildings, and wrought iron balconies were much in evidence.

"In my earlier policy statements," resumed Cruz, "I mentioned I wasn't reluctant to talk about money or women."

"So I noticed." He dodged a peglegged lizardman who came lurching along.

"It occurs to me that the wife of our client may once have played a somewhat important part in your life."

"She did."

Cruz smoothed his moustache with real fingers. "Is that likely to affect this undertaking in any way?"

"Nope."

"Keeping all your glum thoughts to yourself isn't always the best—"

"Do you ever talk to yourself?"

"Rarely. I usually have no trouble rustling up an attentive audience."

"I do. Did anyway," said Smith. "I talked to myself . . . seems like it was for months. I talked to myself about Jennifer and what happened until there isn't anything more I feel like saying. Even to me."

Cruz' broad shoulders rose and fell. "Should the situation change."

A few yards up ahead, a pair of swinging doors snapped suddenly wide open. Three apemen in checkered suits, a cocktail robot, a stuffed blue parrot and most of a full course fish dinner came flying out into the street.

Nodding at the flapping doors, Smith said, "This is the place we want."

10 ══════════════════

The owner of the Cafe Frisco brushed his knuckles on one spotless lapel of his two-piece white tuxsuit. He was a middlesized human, sandyhaired and roughhewn, about forty. "Anybody else got any complaints about the soup du jour?" he inquired of the patrons of the main dining area.

One of the two pale lizard bishops at the table nearest him said, in a subdued voice, "Actually, sir, lukewarm is much nicer than hot. As we were about to point out to the unfortunate gentlemen who just left."

"And these floating blobs of grease," added his colleague, "enhance the flavor."

"Rocky!" shouted the big catman bartender. "Behind youse!"

Rocky Jordan spun, gracefully, to meet the attack of the pair of angry spacewallopers who'd come charging out of one of the gaming rooms.

Dodging deftly, he slugged one and then the other, both square on the jaw.

The men, both big shaggy fellows, collapsed and fell onto the remains of the table that had been occupied by the catmen who'd been unhappy with their Plutonian Gumbo.

Jordan wiped the palms of his hands on his immaculate white trousers. "Thanks, Chris," he called to the grinning bartender.

"Drink, Rocky?"

"The usual."

"One sparkling water with a twist of chokaa coming up."

"Even these fat unidentified bugs swimming in our tepid soup are a delightful addition," said one of the bishops. "We have nary a complaint, Mr. Jordan."

"Those are cockroaches," said Jordan. "Anything you want to know about our recipes, just ask. But politely." He nodded to the huge snakeman near the doorway. "Haul these gents out into the sunshine and fresh air, Sam." He poked one of the unconscious gamblers with his foot.

When Jordan reached the bar, Smith walked over to him. "Hi, Rocky."

Stiffening, the cafe proprietor brought up both hands. "Damn, it's Jared Smith," he said, relaxing and smiling.

"This is Cruz," said Smith. "We're working on something."

"Yeah, for Whistler. I heard." Jordan leaned an elbow on the bar. "Buy you guys a drink?"

"Sparkling water," said Smith.

"Same," said Cruz.

"Whoops, my dear," snickered a cyborg at the other

end of the bar. "Two more pansies heard from."

"Friend," advised Chris the bartender, "you better bid everybody farewell and gather up your effects."

"Huh?"

"You're leaving."

"No, I'm waiting here to meet a chap who's going to sell me a tenant's insurance policy for my desert yurt . . . ooofooo!"

Jordan had lifted him clear off his stool. After tossing him aside, he said, "One more for the egress, Sam, when you get the time."

"Gar!" A huge lizard stormtrooper popped up out of his chair. "What in the blue blazes is the big idea, Jordan? I don't mind a little broken crockery in my Waldorf salad, but I resent your dropping this gink smack in my tub of avocado dip."

"Are you complaining?" Jordan eyed him.

"Well, not exactly."

"Sit down then."

"Okay, but . . . well, listen, Rocky, my mother brought me up to be a fastidious eater," explained the big green man as he settled into his chair. "Having a stranger's nose and chin resting in my dip makes me uneasy. Fact is, I doubt the health department would want me to dunk my rice crackers into this stuff now that—"

"Chris, have Susan bring this gent a fresh bowl of dip. On the house." He sauntered back to the bar. "Can I help you, Jared?"

"I'm hoping so."

"I can try."

Cruz was glancing around the big room, taking in the customers and then the view of the canal you got through the high tinted windows. "I heard you were tough, Jordan, but . . ."

"I'm a little cranky today," explained the owner. "It's the height of the pollen season and that always riles me. Most other times I'm gentle as . . . what are you staring at, buddy?"

A handsome cleancut blond young man in a three-piece travelsuit had stepped in out of the bright day. He had three cameras dangling around his sunburned neck and a slim blonde young woman on his arm. "Sorry, if I'm annoying you, Mr. Jordan. It is Mr. Jordan, isn't it?"

"Yeah. So?"

"I'm Wilson Teanegg, Jr. From Mars in the Earth System," the young man explained, smiling nervously and guiding his companion closer to the bar. "This is my lovely wife Wanita . . . don't step on that man, dear. We're on a tour and . . . well, we've heard so much about you that I was wondering if I could get a picture of you. Here in your natural habitat, so to speak."

"I guess so." Jordan was frowning. "One picture."

"Gee, thanks. That's swell. Isn't it, Wanita?"

"It's really terrific."

Cruz rubbed at his nose with his metal forefinger, studying the couple.

"This'll only take a second, Mr. Jordan." Smiling, Teanegg raised one of his cameras and clicked off a picture. "Thanks a million."

After he and his wife had departed Smith asked, "What's the matter, Cruz?"

"Something about that guy . . ."

"Most tourists are strange," observed Jordan.

Cruz drummed on the bartop with his real fingers for a few seconds. "I ran into somebody like him before," he said. "Yes, it was while I was pursuing the wife of a used android dealer over on the planet Tarragon in the Barnum System. He called himself Crackpot Charlie, this dealer, and insisted his wife go around telling all and sundry her name was Mrs. Crackpot Charlie. At the time I came along to brighten her life she—"

"Does this lusty narrative have some point?" asked Smith, reaching for his just-arrived sparkling water.

"It does indeed." Cruz nodded toward the doorway. "I'm pretty certain Crackpot had several fellows just like Brother Teanegg in stock."

"In stock?"

"They call them Alfies," continued Cruz. "Which stands for Artificial Life Form. They're youthful looking humanoids that haven't been on the market for several years. Used to be manufactured by—"

"Syndek," finished Smith. "Triplan's chief rivals. This lad was disguised some, but you could be right."

"Why the heck," inquired Jordan, "would a sinth want a picture of me?"

"He wanted us," said Smith.

From the high, wide one-way window of Jordan's private office you could see the vast gambling casinos across the canal shimmering in the afternoon sunlight.

"More of them than ever," observed Smith from his lucite hiphug chair.

"Those new bastards over there have no ethics." Jordan was perched on the edge of his tin desk, his dangling right leg swinging slowly to and fro. "Take the way they run the Fatal Illness room, for instance. It's a sin and a—"

"That's a new game to me," said Smith.

"You bet," put in Cruz, who was standing near the window, "on the exact second a terminally ill patient'll die. It's a variation on the old Teenage Orgasm dodge."

"Leaving the poor taste angle out of it," said Jordan,

"these bozos get my grout with the way they fake things. Hell, last week they rang in a zombie as the patient. Two nights ago they planted a resurrectionist in the crowd, bringing some withered old biddy back to life on the sly every time she croaked. You can make a stewpot of profit off gambling without resorting to cheating or sorcery."

Smith said, "We're looking for a fellow named Oscar Ruiz."

Gesturing at the pleasure domes across the hazy water of the Grand Canal, the Cafe Frisco owner said, "Ruiz used to work in the Faulty Parachute room over in Mac-Quarrie's Pavillion. You know, that's where you bet on whether a skydiver's chute'll open or not. Never thought that one was much fun."

"Especially for the divers. Did Ruiz quit?"

"Three weeks back, yeah."

"We'd like to know where he is now."

"So would MacQuarrie."

Cruz asked, "He skip with some funds?"

"A hundred thousand trubux."

"Any idea where he is?" said Smith.

Jordan wandered around behind his desk, sat on the edge of his tin swivel chair. "I've never much cared for MacQuarrie," he said finally. "Which is why I didn't bother to mention to the bastard that I happened to find out about Ruiz' present whereabouts."

"But you know where he is?"

Jordan answered, "The guy went on a pilgrimage to the Shrine."

"You were right," Cruz said to Smith.

"Ruiz didn't come back," said Jordan. "Instead he holed up at a place called the Red Desert Oasis. A tourist trap."

"Didn't MacQuarrie's boys look for him there?"

"Hell, yes, but not in the right places." Jordan pointed at the floor. "Ruiz is under the joint. There's a hideaway setup under there that very few people know about. Expensive."

Smith said, "Heard of anyone else looking for Ruiz?"

"Gent from Triplan, couple weeks back." Jordan shook his head. "You wouldn't believe how small their bribes are."

"You tell him anything?"

"Quite a few things, none of them true. Hell, for a lousy thousand trubux you don't get the truth. Not from Rocky Jordan."

"Besides Triplan, anyone else?"

Jordan smiled. "This is about more than a missing hundred grand, isn't it?"

"Yep, it is."

"Our old buddy, Deac Constiner."

"When?"

"Yesterday."

"Think he found out anything?"

"Not from me, and I'm just about the only one who knows where Ruiz is holed up."

Cruz stroked his metal arm. "We ought to take bets," he suggested. "Who's going to find Oscar Ruiz first."

"My dough's on you and Smith," said Jordan.

11

The plump blonde woman giggled. "That's absolutely marvelous," she told Jack Saint.

"Yes, isn't it, rather?"

"I'm not at all musical myself."

"Ah, I find that deuced hard to believe, Esme."

They were drifting along a quiet, treelined stream in a plaz gondola. A metal-bodied twelve-string guitar was floating in the air some three feet above the green man's dapper lap, seemingly plucking itself.

Esme sighed contentedly, letting a plump hand trail over the robotpowered gondola edge into the water. "This is, beyond doubt, the most wonderful lunch break I've ever spent since I began work in the Confidential Records Department of Triplan nine weary years ago."

"Jove, you must've commenced your drudgery while still a wee babe," he said.

"I'm a bit older than you imagine, Jiggs."

He'd told her, when he manufactured a meeting last night on the esplanade, that his name was Jiggs Sandington. "The years have been kind to you then, my dear."

"May I confess something to you?"

"Do, dear girl," he invited.

"Until I met you, I'd never dated anyone who was . . . um . . . tinted as you are." Esme lowered her eyes. "Mostly because I didn't think I would go well with green, because of my blondeness. Wasn't that silly of me?"

"All I can say is that I'm deuced glad you overcame your qualms."

She said, "I've never cared much for men with red hair either. Yet, in your case, Jiggs . . ."

"My hair is orange."

"Orange, red. You know what I mean."

"One hesitates to state the obvious," Saint said, letting the guitar settle into the bottom of their gently drifting craft, "yet an inborn honesty compels me to point out, fair lady, that love knows no boundaries."

After giggling yet again, she said, "You know, that's absolutely true. Because I didn't even much fancy short men until you came into my life. No matter what color they were, since I'm rather a tall, fullfigured woman myself."

"Actually, Esme dear, I'm not short," Saint clarified. "If you take the height of all the myriad denizens of the universe into account, then the average male is only four foot six."

"He really must be a shrimp," said Esme. "You're taller than that, aren't you?"

"By nearly a foot, yes."

"Well, it just goes to show what my grandmother used to say. 'Never judge a vombis by its snoog.' "

"What does that mean precisely?"

"Well, it's supposed to indicate that . . . I'm not exactly sure what a vombis is, but they had scads of them on the planet where granny grew up."

"Some sort of beast, eh?"

Esme rubbed at her dimpled chin. "I think so, unless it's a vegetable," she replied. "Granny was a vegetarian in her final years and a good many of her maxims had a vegetable slant. Anyway, the proverb sort of means, the way she used it, that someone may well be repulsive on the outside but marvelously attractive on the inside."

"Thank you so much."

She sighed, blushing. "I swear I'm all tongue-tied today," she said. "What I mean is, even though you're little and green, I'm quite fond of you. You've been so nice and attentive, without trying to put your little green hands on the more intimate parts of my body. A girl likes that in a man. I also appreciate the way you took the time, when you picked me up at the office for lunch, to allow me to show you around the Confidential Records offices and even the Top Secret Room. Most men never ever take that much interest in me or my work."

"To me, don't you see, old girl, everything you do is of the utmost interest." He reached over to take hold of her hand, the one that had been dragging in the stream.

"This is marvelous," Esme said contentedly. "I'm glad fate brought us together."

"It wasn't fate," murmured Saint as he kissed her pudgy fingers.

Saint wasn't interested in the window display. In fact, he found it quite difficult to understand why anyone would be at all desirous of feasting his or her eyes on the nearly lifesize automatons that were cavorting therein. Simulacra of a quartet of lizardwomen they were, decked out in neon-trimmed gowns and mouthing the lyrics of the tune that was blasting forth from the talkboxes overhead.

"Beat me, daddy, with a solid jive. . . ."

Wincing, Saint took another careful glance back the way he'd come. Yes, the lean chap in the ill-fitting two-piece canal-blue cazsuit had halted three shop windows behind him.

"Let me see," thought Saint, "is the bloke with the Trinidad Law Bureau, Syndek . . . or is he interested in one of my earlier escapades?"

Didn't really matter much, the chap had to be shaken off.

After patting his bright orange hair, Saint resumed his stroll.

Up ahead, an escalator walkway led down to another level of the mall.

"Poor lad's going to take rather a nasty spill."

Saint was halfway down the escalator when the man who was tailing him stepped on it. Concentrating, he caused the shadow's right foot to fly out from under him.

"Yow," he heard the man cry out as he fell over onto the chubby birdwoman in front of him.

Before everyone was untangled, Saint was far away.

Safe in his hotel room, certain no eavesdropping devices had been introduced while he was gone, Saint settled into a comfortable rubber armchair. Crossing his legs, steepling his fingers, shutting his eyes, he thought about the layout of the Top Secret Room at Triplan.

Within that room buttons were depressed, orders

were given to various mechanisms and safety checks were overridden. The information Smith required was printed out without anyone's being aware of it. And seconds later it teleported right to Saint's lap.

Letting out his breath, the green man gathered up the dozen pages he'd teleported out of the data storage area of Triplan.

After scanning the first three pages, he said, "Ah, so that's what the blighters are really so anxious about, is it?"

Two pages further along Saint came to the list of the ten former Horizon Kids who carried the secret.

"Jove!" He sat up straight. "This blooming list doesn't quite match the one the lady provided us with. Not exactly, no."

Jared Smith's name was on this one.

12 ═══════════

"More buzzards," observed Cruz, gazing through the passenger side of the landvan windshield. "Two blue ones, three yellow. Death certainly comes in colorful shapes in the Trinidads."

Smith, in the driveseat, said, "Could be they're circling whatever it is that's sending up that column of black smoke yonder."

"The Oasis can't be on fire?"

"We're still about ten miles from there."

Cruz leaned back in his seat. "Are we inquisitive enough to go over and take a gander?"

"Might as well."

After they'd rolled through the hazy desert afternoon for another ten minutes they crested a dune and saw the source of the smoke.

A tourist landbus, sprawled on its side on the orangish sand, was just finishing burning up. Grouped a safe distance away were two dozen pilgrims and tourists.

"What's that godawful wailing?" asked Cruz. "There don't seem to be any dead or wounded."

"It's the Sophisticates." Smith guided their van down toward the cluster of people. "Those four lizardladies on the right there. They're singing."

"Some kind of shock reaction, is it?"

"Nope, I imagine they're trying to boost folks' morale after this accident."

"I note laz holes in the roof of yonder vehicle, indicating this wasn't exactly an accident."

"Somebody strafed them." Smith parked the landvan and stepped out.

" . . . so don't sit under the utumbo tree with anyone else but me," the green quartet was concluding, "till I come marching home."

One of them smiled around at the dusty bedraggled passengers. "What would you like to hear next to cheer you up, dears?"

"Silence," suggested a pudgy catman in a two-piece black clericsuit.

"Girls," said Norman Vincent Bagdad, the lugubrious gentleman who had accosted Smith on the spaceliner, "give everybody a break and pipe down for a while."

"Honestly, Norm, you're not at all supportive of—"

"Hey, look, here comes Smith." Bagdad waved. "What a funny coincidence."

"What happened?" Smith asked.

"We were attacked by a stray strafingdrone," said the catman cleric. "A representative of the idiotic Mizayen Commandos. It's almost a divine miracle we all escaped with our lives."

"No, no," put in a thin man in a candy-striped robe, "it was definitely the Qatzir Militiamen. I noticed the insignia on the belly of the robot ship. Two crossed scimitars on a field of silvery ammo."

"But that isn't the Militiamen insignia," said a motherly greyhaired catwoman. "They use two crossed bayonets on a circle of—"

"You're thinking of the Qatfia Guards, granny."

Cruz nudged Smith, mentioning quietly, "Note the darkhaired lad in the green cazsuit."

"Looks sort of like Teanegg the alfie, in disguise."

"Yeah, it is, or a reasonable facsimile."

Smith asked the group, "Have you signaled for help?"

"All our communications," replied the cleric, "were destroyed when the bus was hit. We've been trying to decide what to do next. Some favored hiking, others prayer or—"

"I'll use our van radio to get you some help."

Cruz meantime was strolling casually around the crowd. Eyes on the colorful circling buzzards, he suddenly lunged and caught Teanegg by the arm.

"Gosh, sir, what's the meaning of—"

"We merely want to have a chat," explained Cruz as he hustled the artificial man over to the landvan.

"I appreciate your attempts at friendliness, but I really don't—"

"Hush," advised Cruz.

Sitting in the cab, Smith was frowning. "Been trying to contact the Oasis," he said, "but nobody's answering."

"Suppose we converse with friend Teanegg and then try again?" Cruz urged the young man up into the passenger seat and remained standing in the doorway with his metal hand on his shoulder.

"Golly, I'm sure glad my lovely wife, Wanita, isn't along on this particular jaunt," he said. "Because I'd hate to have her see me being manhandled.''

"You don't have a wife," Smith told him. "Alfies don't marry."

"Hey, that's a nasty thing to say about a guy. I may be a bit effeminate looking, but that—''

"You're working for Syndek." Cruz touched his metal wrist and a tiny truthbug came snaking out of his metal thumb.

"Ouch," complained Teanegg when the disc was affixed to the base of his skull.

"Now, tell us why you're—''

The artificial man had started to shiver. His perfect teeth were rattling, his eyes watering.

"The bug!" yelled Smith, grabbing at it.

Teanegg stiffened, slumped.

"Shit, too late," said Smith. "He's dead."

Cruz retrieved the bug. "They had him structured to die if somebody tried to question him with any kind of gadget."

"I'm rusty," said Smith. "I should've anticipated that."

They were stopped a quarter-mile short of the Oasis. There was a barricade of spiked plazwire and neowood stretched across the road. Landvans, landcars and sky-hoppers were parked all around on the sands of the desert.

"Must be a media event taking place at the resort," remarked Cruz, driving their landvan off the roadway.

"Sounds like some kind of skirmish." Smith dropped out of the cab.

You could hear the whomp of explosions, the sizzle of kilcannons from the vicinity of their destination.

Because of the rise of the desert the Oasis wasn't visible from here.

A frogman in a one-piece tan armysuit came trotting over to them. "This is a restricted area," he warned, waving his stunrod at them. "No rubbernecking."

"Press," said Cruz, extracting an ID card from a slot in his metal arm. "We're with . . ." He paused to check what was printed on this particular fake card. "With *9Plan News*."

"Here to distort our basic issues and—"

"Who's fighting?" asked Smith.

"We want to make sure," added Cruz, "we give our nine hundred million subscribers a fair account of—"

"Well, a platoon of the vicious Qatzir Militiamen are trapped at the Oasis," said the frog corporal. "Being in the Mizayen Commandos myself, I, naturally, hate them from both a military and religious point of view. Therefore, I'm pleased as punch to be able to report that my comrades in arms are wiping them out. Now, let me fill you in on the basic religious issues behind this present conflict. Firstly, it is our belief, and the only one a right-thinking man can hold, that the Holy Prophet Plaut meant this desert to be—"

"But the Oasis," cut in Smith, "it's being shelled?"

"What's left of it is, yes."

"How much damage?"

"Before the Militiamen fanatics . . ." He spit at his boots. "Before they took up positions there, the Qatfia Guards made an unsuccessful attempt to assassinate Dag Wentim, the acting generalissimo of the Norkin Elite Horse Guards. He escaped, but most of the tennis pavilion and the—"

"To really cover this properly," said Cruz, resting his real hand on the corporal's shoulder, "we ought to get right up close to the fighting."

The frogman shook his head. "Not possible," he told them. "We're only allowing the crew from *Trinidad Wallview News* to move any closer than this. That's their armored newsvan getting ready to roll over there. Our commander feels that only *TWN* will give an unbiased—"

"Ah, but we're affiliated with them," said Cruz. "We'll just pop over there and introduce ourselves."

"I suppose," said the guard, "since you seem intent on giving us a fair shake, there's no harm in allow-ing—"

"None at all," Smith assured him.

The middle-aged catwoman in the one-piece khaki cazsuit was saying, "Norbert, don't be a ninny."

"But, Mom," the chubby cat newsman said, digging the toe of his combat boot into the reddish sand beside the newsvan, "this really isn't my strong suit."

She caught hold of both his arms just above his fuzzy elbows. "This is the brink of the big time, sonny," she said. "The making of Norbert Willow, the forging in the fire of combat of an ace newscaster, the—"

"Mom, listen, they sent me out here by mistake," protested Willow. "The computer fouled up the orders and if you hadn't insisted that we—"

"You have to grab opportunities when they—"

"Who the heck—I mean honestly, Mom—wants the opportunity to get his backside shot off?"

"There's no need to talk dirty. Besides, you're going to be inside this nice safe van with thick armor." Reaching out, she thunked the side of the *TWN* vehicle with her calico fist. "Safe as houses, sonny."

"What I usually do, Mom, for the *Trinidad Wallview News* outfit is help run the fundraising auctions for our educational channel," protested the furry broadcaster. " 'Folks, here we have a lovely pair of Venusian anti-macassars. Remember that your bids and pledges help bring you the great programming such as tonight's marvelous old tri-op flick *I Slept With A Watermelon*, starring—' "

"Are you really content to do that for the rest of your life?"

Willow nodded vehemently. "I surely am, Mom, you bet," he answered. "It's a darn lot better than being maimed by some crackbrained religious zealots who . . ."

Cruz and Smith moved around the bickering mother and son team, heading for the open doorway of the big gunmetal landvan.

From inside came a sudden groan and curse.

"Oh, I'm sorry, Mr. Merloo. I thought that was your plaz foot I stepped on."

"Right's plaz, left's still real, bimbo."

"Sorry," apologized a sweet feminine voice.

Cruz and Smith climbed up into the van.

A one-eyed lizardman in a two-piece paramilitary caz-suit was hopping on one foot in front of a robotcamera. A slim blonde young woman, carrying a small portable voxunit, was watching.

"What the futz do you want, greaseball?" the lizard-man asked Cruz.

Cruz smiled cordially. "It's a pleasure meeting a famed war correspondent like you."

"Obviously it is," agreed Merloo, his visible eye nar-rowing. "But that doesn't explain why you and that skinny gink have come barging into my van, does it now?"

"Balls Merloo," said Smith, feigning awe, "my boy-hood idol."

The blonde was making anxious shooing motions at them. "Shoo, shoo," she mouthed. "Flee."

"We're hitching a ride," explained Cruz.

"In a grout's valise," said Balls Merloo, adjusting his plaid eyepatch with his plaz left hand.

"Dread," murmured the blonde, hugging the voxunit tightly to her chest. "He's going to erupt."

"The situation is this," said Smith, grinning. "We have to get to the Oasis and you're just about the only available means of transport."

"Oh, yeah? Well, you're wrong there, buster," Merloo informed him. "Because I'm going to summon two big vicious goons on my staff and have them kick your skinny ass all the way there."

"Horrors," said the shivering young woman.

"Tell you what," the one-eyed newsman said to Cruz. "I have a sweet and kindly side to me. So I'm going to count all the way up to five before I knock you on your flabby keester. One—"

"Wait now." Cruz held out his metal hand toward the correspondent. "You really ought to take a gander at this, since you have a fake arm yourself."

"I'm in no flapping mood to admire some halfassed crip's prosthetic—"

Zzzzzzzummmmmm!

The thin stunbeam had come humming out of Cruz' middle finger to hit the lizardman smack in the chest.

Balls Merloo dropped right down to the van floor, his various artificial portions producing assorted clicks, clangs and thunks.

"Calamity," said the blonde, still shaking.

Smith moved to the doorway, caught the handle of the open door. "Good news, Norbert," he called out before tugging it shut. "You won't have to go, after all."

13 ================================

"Would it be all right if I were to introduce myself?" asked the blonde timidly as the newsvan went barreling along across the desert. "Since we seem to be sharing all this adversity together."

Cruz was driving the borrowed vehicle. "Forgive our rudeness, fair lady," he said. "I'm Cruz."

"Jared Smith." He'd just finished dragging Merloo's unconscious body behind a tape-editing unit.

"I'm Jazz Miller," she said, finally setting the vox-unit aside. "Kind of a dippy name, isn't it?"

"On the contrary," said Cruz. "It has a nice lilt to it."

Jazz shrugged. "It's always struck me as an unfortunate handle."

"Change it," advised Smith as he took the passenger seat next to Cruz.

"Oh, no, I couldn't ever do that. Daddy would hate

that. That'd produce a real misfortune," she said. "He's miffed enough as it is because of my chosen profession."

Smith asked, "Which is?"

"Oh, I'm sorry. I didn't tell you, did I? I'm an associate newscaster. Thus far that's involved mostly schlepping equipment and avoiding Mr. Merloo's passes."

"Would you like to cover the conflict at the Oasis?" said Smith.

She pressed her hands to her stomach. "I . . . I don't know if I'm ready."

"Sure you are," said Cruz.

"Merloo's unable to function," Smith pointed out. "You have to step in."

Cruz added, "It's the brink of the big time."

"Actually," she said, slowly and thoughtfully, "I do know a heck of a lot more about the local political situation than Mr. Merloo does. I was saying to my old Poli Sci prof, Doctor Winiarsky, just last week—"

"Hey, would that be Bryson Winiarsky?" cut in Smith.

"Yes, do you know him or . . . oh, rack and ruin. I wasn't supposed to blab about him."

"He's on our list," realized Cruz.

"Yep, and supposedly vanished."

"He's only just hiding out," said Jazz. "Because he got the notion certain people mean him no good. He and I are rather close, which is why I—"

"People do mean him harm," said Smith. "But I think we can prevent his getting knocked off or even seriously hurt."

She studied him. "I hope you don't mind my saying this, Mr. Smith," she said. "But your face doesn't exactly inspire faith and confidence in me."

"He's trustworthy," said Cruz.

"You I can believe in, Mr. Cruz. Therefore, I suppose if you vouch for him, then—"

An enormous explosion sounded outside, and the van shook and wobbled.

"Let's save the character reference stuff," said Smith. "We've arrived at our destination."

" . . . the scene here is one of mishap and calamity. The once proud and palatial resort that bloomed here amidst the harsh starkness of the mighty Red Desert, in the very shadow, as it were, of the planet-renowned Shrine, now stretches out before our unbelieving eyes, smoking ruin. Dedicated Qatzir Militiamen are locked in mortal combat with equally dedicated Mizayen Commandos amidst the pathetic pile that was once the majestic Oasis Dinner Theater and . . ."

From a weaponproof glaz booth up in the domed roof of the parked newsvan, Jazz was describing the battle going on in front of them. A robot camera was prowling outside, circling the fighting.

Smith was crouched, lifting a round panel in the van floor.

"You've still got to cover maybe ten yards in the open out there," said Cruz.

"But not where they're fighting."

"The way these exuberant lads do battle, a stray shot from a kilrifle might—"

"The trapdoor to the underground hideaway ought to be directly beyond that hunk of wall yonder," said Smith. "I'll drop out, scoot over there and get below to Ruiz."

"May well be that everybody in that underground nook is dead and done for, old chum."

"Place is supposed to be fortified, according to Rocky Jordan."

"Well, okay." Shrugging one shoulder, Cruz went back to the driveseat. "Good luck."

Nodding once, Smith dropped down to the broken ground beneath the newsvan.

Smith raised a swirl of dust when he hit. Since he only had about three feet of clearance under the van, he had to belly along over the rubble.

When he reached the nose of the vehicle, he took a cautious look out from under.

Some three hundred yards to the left two dozen commandos were strung out, firing at the Oasis casino. Their kilrifles sizzled and crackled in the desert air.

Part of the front wall of the plaz and glaz casino suddenly came exploding out. Besides thousands of glittering shards, hundreds of playing cards fluttered and scattered across the rutted courtyard.

Smith turned his attention on his destination. The trapdoor entrance he wanted was just on the other side of the rear wall of what had been the cocktail lounge's storeroom. The fighting made Smith's task easier in one sense—he wouldn't have to break into the place. All he had to do was jump over the remainder of the wall, which was less than four feet high.

He waited, watching and listening. Then he eased out into the open and rose to a crouch. The two opposing factions, intent on wiping each other out, didn't notice him.

Smith sprinted. He vaulted the brix wall, landing with one booted foot in a tumbled crate of shattered sparkling water flasks. He slipped and slid into a fallen servobot.

" . . . name your poison," gurgled the sprawled mechanism.

Rubbing at his knee, which had bonked against the robot's elbow, Smith edged over to the spot where the hidden door was supposed to be. The freezer that had masked it was splintered in half, its contents, fruitballs and rainbow ices, melting into a colorful slush on the floor.

"Here we are." Spotting the handle, Smith cleared aside debris and rainbow slurp and took hold of it.

He yanked, hard, and the trapdoor came silently open. A curving ramp led down to the hidden level below.

Smith stepped onto it and descended. When he closed the door behind him, all the furor of the battle died away.

14 ═══════════════

The six-armed green guard held five pistols, all aimed at Smith. With his sixth hand he was wiping at his tearful eyes with a plyochief. "Come no farther, pal," he advised.

Recognizing the green man, Smith said, "How long've you been working here, Sadsack?"

Lowering his plyochief and shifting his grip on his three kilguns, one lazgun and one stungun, Sadsack Swingle eyed him. "Jared Smith . . . what brings you to this cesspool of iniquity?"

"Paying a call on an old school chum."

"Fine day you picked," said Swingle in his mournful voice. "Bands of crazed zealots clashing up above our very heads. This once proud resort complex a smoldering ruin and the pollen count the highest it's been in weeks. You maybe don't think there's much pollen in the desert, but the damn winds across the—"

"Looking for Oscar Ruiz."

"That sourpuss." Swingle shook his head. "You know what really gets my grout is a guy who's all the time complaining. Granted living down here is about three steps worse than residing in a sewer, but even so there's no reason to—"

"Ruiz is still around?"

"Where could the poor sap go? They'd hunt him like a snerg if he ever fled the sanctuary of—"

"Where can I find him?"

Gesturing with the hand that held the stungun, Swingle said, "Down that corridor on the left. Geeze, they've got a lousy aircirc system in that one. Instead of filtering out gunk, it sucks in pollen, spores—"

"You given up your career?"

"I had to," answered the green guard. "When you knew me during your law enforcement days I was struggling to be a successful shoplifter. You'd figure a guy with six arms'd be a natural for that line of work, but I was always the most obvious suspect. I tried to work as a blackjack dealer for Rocky Jordan for a spell, but the customers were always getting the idea I had a card up my sleeve. Basically, it's a mean old world to—"

"I'll drop in on Ruiz."

"He'll squawk. That guy can complain about company or—"

"He won't mind seeing an old friend." Grinning, Smith headed along the corridor with the defective aircirc system.

Smith said, "There's not much upstairs anymore."

Oscar Ruiz said, "So? This setup is self-contained. Two hundred people can live down here indefinitely."

He was a middlesized humanoid of thirty, moderately overweight.

"Consider, then, this aspect of your situation." Smith, arms folded, leaned against a yellow wall of the underground suite's living room. "If I found you, others will."

"Hooey," commented Ruiz from his plaz rocker. "You're better at this sort of thing than most, Jared. It's one of your few real talents, hunting hapless people."

"Guys with a hundred thousand trubux don't qualify as hapless."

"Listen, you think it's fun being a fugitive? Or cheap? If I didn't have my religious faith to sustain—"

"Oscar, it isn't just your chagrined former bosses who're concerned over your present whereabouts," Smith said. "I was hired by people who are interested in you for entirely different reasons."

"So you claim. I've heard, though, that you've been on the skids since Jenny came to her senses and ditched you." Ruiz was ticking slowly back and forth. "For all I know, you've reached such a low peak in your seedy career that you'd even hire out to those bastards at the casin—"

"We weren't especially close at Horizon House, but—"

"You were a loner, didn't make many friends. Except for Jenny, and I was pretty sure you only played up to her so her father, Doctor Westerland, would give you extra little—"

"Oscar, I have to get you out of here quick." Smith moved closer to him. "Before my mode of transportation gets blown up. Gather up your loot and we'll depart."

"No, I'm not interested in decamping. You haven't even really explained why I should risk—"

"Okay, there's one group that wants to get you, find out what you know and then kill you," said Smith evenly. "The Trinidad Law Bureau wants you, too, but I'm not sure if they just mean to detain you or maybe knock you off. Myself, I was hired to bring you back to Horizon House."

"Horizon House? Why the hell would anybody want—"

"Our client claims it's for a reunion, but—"

"Jared, you must be goofy. You think I'd risk my neck, not to mention my hard-earned—"

"I didn't say our client was being completely honest. The truth is you know part of an important secret."

Ruiz blinked. "This doesn't make any—"

"I don't know what the secret is," Smith told him, "and neither do you. It was planted in your skonce, by way of electrohypnosis, by Westerland. Ten Horizon Kids were used."

Slowly Ruiz got to his feet. "What's this client of yours willing to pay me for my part of whatever the hell this is?"

"That you'll have to negotiate."

"You weren't supposed to tell me this part of it, were you, Jared? They're going to be—"

"I'm telling you so you'll realize how important it is to get your ass out of here." Impatience was showing in Smith's voice. "The other lads who want you are much less cordial than I am. When they caught up with Hal Larzon they gathered in his piece of the secret, then killed him."

"Hal? But he and I were pretty close at Horizon House. Not big buddies, but we got along well and . . . he's dead?"

"Yep, and that could happen to you, Oscar."

"Suppose I come with you . . . how do you keep me any safer than—"

"I've got a couple places in mind to stash you," Smith answered before the question was finished. "I'll get you to one of them."

"Doesn't your client want me back as soon as—"

"Since our client hasn't been completely open," said Smith, "I'm using my own judgment until I have more details. The important thing is to keep you, and the other missing Horizon Kids, alive."

"You sound like you really mean what—"

"Pack."

Ruiz took a few deep breaths, glanced around the yellow room. "I never much liked you back then, but you weren't a liar or a conman."

"I'm not now. Let's move."

"All right, okay." Ruiz headed for the door to the bedchamber. "I'll get my gear."

Then the living room door hissed open. "You're not bad," said Deac Constiner from the threshold. "You found this damn nitwit even quicker than I did." He showed Smith the kilgun in his leathery right hand.

15

Ruiz made a gulping sound. "Listen, Constiner," he said, stopped still on the thermocarpet, "I haven't actually committed any crime. What I mean is, taking money from a crook like MacQuarrie, a gambler who fleeced poor—"

"Oscar, Oscar," said the Trinidad Law Bureau agent, "I don't give a snerg's ass about your halfwit dipping into that casino's petty cash."

"As I already mentioned," reminded Smith.

"Nope, I want you for entirely different reasons," said Constiner. He tugged a stungun from beneath his tunic with his left hand. "You, Smith, I don't need, and so—"

"Are you the one, Deac, who caught up with Hal Larzon?"

Snorting, the lawman said, "Don't talk like a schmuck. I don't work that way and neither do you."

Smith said, "If you want Larzon's piece of the puzzle, you've got to find the folks who bumped him off."

"I'll tell you, Smith, this whole frumus is getting to be a pain in the toke," admitted Costiner. "It was already too cute going in and it keeps getting trickier and trickier."

"TLB figures the secret belongs to them and not to Westerland's next of kin?"

"Westerland worked for the three-planet government when he cooked this particular notion up," he replied. "All we're talking about is a simple legal point here. Any invention you come up with while working for somebody is naturally the employer's. Fact is, I'm the only one in this whole mess who has any real right to—"

"Jennifer Westerland doesn't agree with—"

"Aren't you cured of that broad yet? Don't tell me you still believe the crap she—"

"What about me?" intruded Ruiz. "You two are squabbling and cutting up touches while I'm suffering a hell of a lot of anxiety and discom—"

"You're coming with me," Constiner explained, "and Smith's going to stay here." He aimed the stungun at Smith.

Zzzzzzummmmmm!

It was Constiner who stiffened and then fell to the floor.

"Forgive me, one and all." Smiling, Cruz appeared in the doorway where the TLB lawman had been. "I find I sometimes can't resist these melodramatic entrances."

"Allowable under the circumstances," said Smith, stooping to take both guns away from the fallen man.

Ruiz' breath came sighing out. "I take it this guy's on your side, Jared?"

"He is. Cruz, Oscar Ruiz."

Cruz gave him a lazy salute with his metal hand. "Reason I dropped down was to urge one and all to speed things up. The battle is spilling ever closer to our position."

Smith told Ruiz, "Grab your stuff."

"Violence," muttered Ruiz, trotting into his bedchamber, "my whole damn life has been ringed with violence."

16

Jack Saint frowned and his broad green nose wrinkled. He rose from his seat in the nearly empty shuttle ship, extracted his orange display handkerchief from his pocket and dusted the cracked plaz cushion he'd been sitting upon. He squinted down at it disapprovingly, then dusted it once again.

"You can't get rid of the snull," said a middle-aged catwoman two seats behind him.

"Beg pardon?"

"Oh, my." She raised up a paw, gave herself a nudge in the temple. "The *smell*, I meant to say. You probably haven't guessed it yet, but I happen to be a still."

"A what, Madam?"

"Darn, did it again." Another fist to her head. "*Shill*. See, I'm not actually a catwoman. I'm a cleverly contrived simulacrum. I'm an andy."

"I'd already suspected that," Saint informed her. "Principally from the smell of burning wiring you give off, but also from the small pool of machine oil that's leaked out of your left foot since our shuttle lifted off from Zegundo some minutes ago."

"Yes, it's embarrassing at times to be less than perfect."

"I wouldn't know."

"All of us aboard, except for yourself, are androids and robots."

"Why is that, dear lady?" Saint, very gingerly, lowered his buttocks back down on the seat.

"Oh, it's rather shameful in a way. We're here to foot ... um ... I mean, *fool* the poor gullible public," she answered, brushing at a thin swirl of bluish smoke that was commencing to spiral out of one furry ear. "Fact of the matter is, I wonder why you're making this journey to our satellite."

"Ah, it's because I'm a dyed-in-the-neowool robot buff." Saint smiled over his shoulder at her. "I long ago made a pledge to myself that some fine day I'd hop on a shuttle to visit the Museum of Robotics History that orbits this fair planet."

"I hope you won't think me disloyal if I mention that you're wasting your dough, sir."

"How so, my dear?"

"The place is quite rundown," she confided. "Mostly, though I hesitate mentioning it, mostly because of Professor Bunny's peccadillos."

"That would be Professor Montague R. Bunny, the esteemed electronics historian?"

"He's not all that esteemed anymore," she said. "And don't you feel, by the way, that it's a little late, when a man is pushing sixty-six, to go through midlife crisis?"

"We none of us know when our final moment will

come." Saint elevated his backside, giving the seat another swipe with his handkerchief. "If, for instance, Professor Bunny lives to be one hundred and thirty-two, then—"

"He won't make it to sixty-seven if he continues to pursue nubile maidens with the zeal and brio he's been exhibiting the past few years."

"Perhaps it's difficult for you, being a mechanism," observed Saint, "to comprehend how deuced distracting the urges of the flesh can be."

"Having oil leaking out of your darn foot is no bed of meeches either. If the professor wasn't so neglectful I could hold up my head and—"

Karump! Whamp! Kabump!

The shuttle had docked, none too smoothly, in the landing bay of the orbiting museum.

Saint left his seat, then bent gracefully to fetch his sewdohyde attaché case from beneath it. The case had acquired an unsightly gob of gum on its underside. "Aren't you disembarking?" he inquired of the imitation catwoman while disdainfully plucking the wad of greenish stuff off the case with a plyochief.

"Oh, no, I just ride this thing back and forth all the live-long day. That's what a shull . . . *shill* does, you know."

"One's heart goes out to you." Bowing politely, Saint went striding along the corridor and out of the shuttle.

There was only what appeared to be a slim blonde young woman on the vast welcoming platform. Head tilted a bit forward, eyes slightly narrowed, she was watching his approach. "I'm sorry, but would you be Mr. Saint?"

He considered the question as he scrutinized her.

"Why do you ask, my child?"

The blonde blushed, looking down at herself. "Am I unzipped, unseamed, unbuttoned or something? You're staring at my body as though—"

"I was marveling at your believability," he explained. "Yes, you're a much better work than those rather forlorn androids aboard the—"

"Oh, hey, heck. I'm not a robot or an andy. I'm Jazz Miller and Mr. Smith sent me down to fetch you and escort you up to him, Mr. Saint," Jazz said, smiling. "Actually, he would've come himself, but I felt that since I'm tagging along on this venture, for reasons of my own that we can go into later if you're at all interested, I ought to earn my keep."

Reaching out and catching hold of the young woman's hand, Saint bowed and kissed it. "It's a distinct pleasure, my dear, to meet you."

Blushing again, Jazz slowly withdrew her hand from his. "Mr. Smith mentioned you'd be like this. Courtly and polite."

"He described me to you, eh?"

"Yes," she replied, nodding. "If you'll come along now I'll take you to where everybody's waiting."

"How exactly did he describe my appearance? Did he use such words as dapper, winning, attractive—"

"He just said you were green," said Jazz.

Smith was pacing the cleared area at the center of the storeroom. "Those assholes," he said, the pilfered pages Saint had brought fluttering in his hand.

"Be more specific," requested Cruz, who was sitting in a lamé slingchair with his booted feet up on a neo-wood packing crate labeled *Tapdancing Androids/ One Pair*.

"Hell, I don't know," Smith said. "Triplan first off. They made up a false damn list for—"

"Not logical, old man," Saint pointed out. "They'd have to give the Whistler Agency the true list. Otherwise, don't you know, they wouldn't be certain of getting hold of you."

"They could've told the Whistler folks to hire me, insisted on it," said Smith. "Once I brought in the missing alums, they'd pump what I know out of my head and—"

"My feeling would be our bosses know considerably more than they've thus far confided," commented Cruz. "They went to a hell of a lot of effort to recruit you. Granted you're a splendid operative, but they probably could've found a good one right here on Zegundo."

"Yep, I think the agency knew, too."

Saint stood up to dust the seat of his slingchair a second time. "One feels deuced awkward asking this, old fellow," he said. "Yet one feels one must. Why aren't you considering Jennifer Westerland Arloff's part in all this?"

"I am." Halting, Smith sat on a crate. "She lied to me when we had our stroll along the ocean. And she gave me a fake list, too."

"Look on the bright side," suggested Cruz.

Smith slapped the handful of papers. "What bright side would that be?"

"She was concerned enough to tell you something of the real purpose of our treasure hunt," Cruz said. "Further, she warned you it could well be a lot rougher than you'd been led to believe up to that point."

"You're too sentimental when it comes to women."

Cruz shook his head. "What I've learned in a colorful and fun-filled life, old chum, is most people do the best they can with what they've got," he said. "Jennifer can't . . . and I've no idea why . . . do more than she did. Therefore you have to accept what—"

"It's a little hard to accept her not telling me that I'm carrying part of a secret worth . . . hell, billions of trubux . . . around in my skull."

"She's married to Arloff and his goals aren't yours."

Standing, Smith held the papers out toward Cruz. "Westerland came up with a cheap transmutation process," he said. "A simple way to turn base metals into valuable metals for a cost of just about nothing. Whoever ends up with the whole secret . . . Triplan, Syndek or the Trinidad government . . . they'll be able, if they go carefully, to become as rich as they want. Because this is something that can be utilized and exploited in different ways all over the universe."

Saint asked, "What exactly is our position at the moment? Are we still working for the Whistler blokes?"

"What I'm trying to figure out, and that's why I've got Ruiz stashed here, is what comes next," answered Smith.

"I'd be interested in hearing about that, too, Smitty." The Whistler terminal had materialized a few feet to his left.

17

"You don't have a trusting nature," said Whistler. "A handicap such as that can seriously—"

"You folks have lied to me from the—"

"Nope, not so," said the floating terminal. "First off, take a squint of this, Smitty." It whirred faintly and then a sheet of faxpape came fluttering out of its underside.

Smith caught the sheet before it hit the storeroom floor. "List of five names. Oscar Ruiz, Bryson Winiarsky, Annalee Kitchen, Liz Vertillion and Thomas Yanayir," he said. "This is the same list you gave me when I signed on to—"

"What you hold in your mitt is a dupe of the very list Triplan gave us," said the terminal. "Compare it with the typography on that stuff Saint swiped."

Smith did. "Okay, they match."

"Furthermore, Triplan never told us anything about a secret process for making gold, silver and what have you," continued Whistler. "Not being dimwits, however, we realized there was more to this caper than a sentimental urge to get the old gang together again. We told you so at the start, so did Doc Winner."

Cruz shifted his feet atop the crate. "You contend you didn't know that Jared and not this Yanayir lad was the one they wanted?"

"We were only told it was important to have Smith work on the case, not that—"

Tippy tap tap! Tap tap tappy!

Saint sat up straight. "Jove! What's that deucedly odd noise?"

Cruz kicked the crate and the sound ceased. "Must be my tapdancing androids awakening. Continue, Whistler."

"You galoots are blaming us for the duplicities the client pulled," the computer terminal told them.

"Even so," said Smith, "I don't see how I can keep on working for you."

"Whyever not, Smitty?"

"Because what I want to do is find the three others on this damn list," he explained. "Tell them what's going on, keep them from getting grabbed or killed. Then we can see about making a deal with Triplan."

"You can cross Annalee Kitchen off the list, by the way."

"She's dead, too?"

"No, fit as a fiddle and happy as a snerg," replied Whistler. "It's only that the lady walked into Horizon House late yesterday and announced she'd heard they were looking for her."

Smith said, "Then maybe she's safe."

Watching the floating terminal, Cruz inquired, "You won't bitch if the three of us keep on with the hunt? Doing it Jared's way?"

"We were paid our fee long since," Whistler answered. "And we've been treated badly by our client. Do what you want to do and we'll stay on the sidelines and observe. If it looks like you're doing something too shady, we'll pop in on you."

After a few seconds Smith said, "Okay, it's a deal."

"Just because some people call us Suicide, Inc.," said Whistler, "doesn't mean we can't be amiable." He flickered and vanished.

18

"I'm sorry, but I guess I better tell you this right off, Mr. Cruz," said Jazz, watching the rainy misty afternoon their skycar was whizzing through. "Since we two will be alone together for a spell."

Cruz was in the driveseat of their aircraft. "You can confide anything you like in me." He reached out to bestow a friendly pat on her nearest knee.

"Yikes!" Jazz swung her leg out of the way and Cruz ended up slapping the plaz trim of the passenger seat with his metallic fingers. "That's what I was leading up to. The fact that I'm averse to physical contact of any kind."

"That's sad."

"Well, it's just something you have to learn to live with, as my family physician used to say."

"He didn't touch you either?"

"Oh, him I didn't mind, because he was a robot. It's really only flesh and blood contact that gives me the willies."

"How fortunate for you, then, Jazz, that you ran into me." Smiling, Cruz held up his metal right hand. "You won't be able to tell my deft and delicate touch from that of your trusted medico robot."

She frowned. "I don't know about that, Mr. Cruz. You see, the rest of you is all too human."

"Here, allow me to stroke your cheek and you'll note that—"

"Calamity! You'd best not. I might start screaming and howling, which would distract you from piloting our skycar."

"True." Cruz smiled and dropped his hand. "Duty comes first."

"Are you terribly mad with me? I suppose on most of your adventures and escapades you indulge in all sorts of physical excesses." She folded her hands in her lap. "I do want you to know, Mr. Cruz, that it's not you yourself I find loathsome and disgusting but rather the idea of being touched by you. I wouldn't like that even if you were twice as attractive as you are."

"That puts my mind at ease."

"Besides, even if I enjoyed being pawed and mauled, that's not what I'm here for, is it? No, I'm along to help you establish contact with Professor Winiarsky so you can persuade him to come away with you to the safety of the robot museum."

"You are certain he's at this Jungleland Park we're fast approaching?"

"Unless he's been abducted," answered Jazz with a nod. "I have to apologize for being dense, Mr. Cruz, but I don't think I've got all the opposing forces sorted out yet. I'm not clear on who's trying to kill Winiarsky and who just wants to kidnap him. Fact is, I don't even know for sure why they—"

"Even we aren't completely certain about everything."

"But as a newswoman I ought to be able to unravel—"

"Jazz, this isn't something you're going to be able to report for your network. I explained the sit—"

"I know, this is strictly off the record."

"Exactly."

Sighing, she smiled over at him. "It was nice, don't you think, of the *Trinidad Wallview News* people to give me a leave? Especially after they thought for a while I'd been abducted by rebel forces and that Mr. Merloo was lost in combat and not just dumped in that dry canal next to—"

"They sound like exemplary employees. Now, hold on while I set us down."

She looked out at the swirling mist. "Are we at Jungleland already?"

"We are." Cruz punched out a landing pattern on the control dash.

"It's awfully difficult to tell their artificial jungle from the real jungle surrounding it."

"One good reason, no doubt, why the park has never exactly thrived."

Their skycar landed smoothly on a mossy landing area to the right of the high sewdowood entry gates to Jungleland Park. There were no other vehicles to be seen on the rainswept field.

Jazz was staring out the window. "I wonder if these five men running toward us are friendly," she said. "Those animal skins they're wearing and those clubs and knives they're brandishing make you doubt it, don't they?"

Saint brushed at his nose with his plyochief. "A most fragrant neighborhood, eh?"

He and Smith were walking along a foggy sidestreet in

the Poverty Hollow sector of Metro North, the capital city of this particular Zegundo Territory. The buildings were low, huddled close together, made of brix and glaz. They were grey, dingy, bleaklooking. The derelicts, drunks, mewts, welfs and zanies who shuffled, drifted and staggered by in the yellowish fog all looked moderately familiar to Smith. He realized he might well have been down and out in this very ghetto, although he had no clear recollection of it.

"Liz Vertillion worked in this area up until the time she dropped from sight two months back," Smith said.

A frail bedraggled little girl with three hands held them all out. "Give us a coin."

Saint obliged. "Get yourself some food, child."

"None of your frapping business what I does with it, greenie."

"A pity the blooming universe is so awry," observed Saint as they turned a corner. "No possible way to put things right, eh? Thoughts like that are what drive one into a life of nefarious deeds."

"A true scoundrel wouldn't have given that kid money."

"Perhaps, old man, I'm only conning you with seemingly decent behavior."

Smith nodded. "There's the mission where Liz was working."

"Deuced inspiring name. Last Faint Hope Mission," said Saint. "Conveniently located twixt the Skullpop Saloon and the Lower Depths Diner."

As they moved by the swinging doors of a saloon, a three-eyed blue mewt looked out.

"Bless me! It's old Smith," he chuckled. "Ain't seen you in a grout's age, pal."

Smith paused, studied the mewt. "Hi, Trio. How've you been?"

"Can't complain. All your drinking buddies miss

you, though.'' He narrowed all three eyes. ''You've took a rise in the world. And you're buddying with a real swell. You happy?''

''Happier.'' Smith waved and moved on.

Saint said, ''One hadn't realized how low you'd sunk.''

''I don't even exactly remember coming back to this planet,'' admitted Smith. ''I wandered around quite a bit for a while.''

'' 'Twould be ironic if you'd once been plucked out of the gutter by the now missing Lieutenant Liz Vertillion of the Salvation Squad.''

''Think that would've stuck in my memory.'' Smith reached out to push open the narrow neowood door of the narrow brixfront mission building.

They entered into a low, beam-ceilinged dining room. Only about half of the ten long bare tables were in use.

A rusty cyborg huddled at the farthest table came rattling to his feet. ''Smitty,'' he hailed in a thin, rough-edged voice. ''It's been a spell.''

The gaunt man's name came back to Smith. It was Scrapyard Slim. ''Good to see you again, Slim.''

''You're looking good, Smitty. Like you picked youself up.''

''Had a little help.'' Smith, trailed by Saint, crossed the steamy room. ''Is Lietuenant Zucco around?''

Slim pointed with his pitted chrome left hand. ''Back in the kitchen you'll find him,'' he said. ''The soupmaker's on the fritz again.''

''Thanks.'' They went through the doorless doorway.

''Ah, the memories of thousands of past kettles of soup linger,'' said Saint, touching his plyochief to his round nose.

Squatting in front of a robotstove, a spanner in one furry hand, was a thin catman in a one-piece nightblue Salvation Squad unisuit. ''Smith, isn't it? We've missed you these past months. You appear, however, to have been eating well.''

"Lieutenant, we're looking for Liz Vertillion."

Rising gradually up, Zucco said, ''Several people have been seeking her.'' He touched a wide bandage on his fuzzy forehead. ''One of them was rather persistent in his inquiries.''

"I don't remember much about my last stay on Zegundo," Smith told him, ''and I have no idea what you think of me. But I'm trying to find Liz before somebody kills her.''

Lieutenant Zucco said, ''You may be too late, Jared.''

"Hell, she isn't dead?''

"I truly fear she may be,'' the catman answered. ''Just before she disappeared two months since, she'd antagonized Boss Nast.''

"Who might he be?'' asked Saint. ''The bloke who looks after all the crime and graft hereabouts?''

"That's he. Liz was concerned about some garment sweatshops he owns and . . . I fear she may have been too outspoken in her criticism.''

Smith asked, ''Did you tell the other inquirers this?''

"I did not, no. And none of them bothered to use truth drugs or devices on me, being satisfied that violence would provide all the information I contained.''

"These chaps may well have found out about Boss Nast elsewhere,'' mentioned Saint, who was squinting into the kettle that held the soup of the evening.

"Nevertheless,'' said Smith. ''we'll look the gent up.''

"He's dangerous,'' cautioned the Salvation Squad lieutenant.

"At this point,'' said Smith, ''so am I.''

19

Metal hand and real hand held out palm foremost, Cruz emerged from the skycar cabin. "Gents, this is a peaceable mission we're embarked upon," he assured the surrounding band of junglemen. "No need to cudgel or—"

"See, Kaanga? I told you we were coming on too strong," said one of the junglemen who'd charged across the clearing.

"But isn't that what they expect, Samar? What I'm saying is, the public expects jungle heroes such as us to be ferocious and—"

"Ferocious is one thing. Scaring the billybounce out of them is—"

"Fellas," cut in Cruz, "am I to assume you mean us no harm?"

"Oh, heck," said Jazz from the skycar doorway, "I recognize them now. They're just here for the Jungle-con."

"Isn't that why you people dropped in?" asked the large blond Kaanga.

"Not exactly, no," said Cruz. "We want to visit someone who resides here at Jungleland."

Samar kicked at the sward with his bare foot. "What a flop this convention is turning out to be. I left a lot of responsibilities in my home jungle to come here and be a Guest of Honor," he said. "I had a party of black-hearted ivory hunters to scare off, a lost city to find, not to mention—"

"You know who all these lads are?" Cruz asked the young woman quietly.

"Sure, being a newswoman I have to keep up with the celebrities in the Trinidad System," Jazz answered. "Besides Samar and Kaanga, there's Zago, Tabu and Wambi. Wambi's the cute teen with the turban. They're all of them well-known junglemen, or jungleboy in Wambi's case. The park officials hoped having famous jungle personalities here would cause people to come flocking to their convention."

"Seemingly it hasn't worked."

" . . . and wrestle crocodiles," concluded Samar, brushing back his long yellow hair.

"Tell you what," offered Cruz. "If we conclude our business rapidly, why, we'll give your convention a quick look-in."

"I even brought my elephants," Wambi said. "Did you ever make a space shuttle flight with three cranky elephants?"

"As a matter of fact," said Cruz, "once, when I was romancing a circus star who billed herself as Princess Pantha the Jungle Queen, I escorted not only three elephants but an entire—"

"Mr. Cruz," reminded Jazz, "we're on a rather tight schedule."

"To be sure." Before she could dodge he gave her a cordial pat on the backside with his real hand.

"Audacious yet simple," remarked Saint as he dusted off the windowsill in the abandoned warehouse prior to resting his elbow on it.

"Sure you can do this?" asked Smith.

Turning away from the view of the twilight canal, Saint said, "For a chap with my telekinetic gift, old man, it's a piece of cake. Once we got ourselves a peek at Boss Nast in his skycar, there was no problem."

Smith glanced at the wide, open doorway of the old warehouse. "Might as well commence then."

The dapper green man rubbed his fingertips across his smooth forehead. "Actually I don't have to materialize that heavy, gaudy vehicle," he explained. "Rather I merely take over the controls and guide it here to our temporary lair."

Saint's eyes gradually closed, his body tensed.

Out on the darkening canal a nukebarge hooted as it went chugging by.

When Smith became aware of the sound of an approaching skycar, he drew out his stungun.

Saint opened his eyes, wiped perspiration from his face. "Our prey arrives, old chap."

A large glittering black skycar came wooshing into the open warehouse to make a thumping, bouncy landing on the neowood planks of the dusty floor. The vehicle was decorated with inset gems on its fenders, wings and bumpers. A large golden *N* was emblazoned on the door of the passenger side.

And in the passenger seat a huge lizardman in a two-piece yellow bizsuit was pounding on the glaz window with both beringed hands. His lean humanoid driver was still struggling with the stubborn controls.

"One feels the need of a bit of privacy." Saint gestured at the overhead door of the warehouse and it clattered shut.

The uniformed driver leapt free of the freshly-arrived skycar, going for a weapon under his coat.

Zzzzzummmmm!

Smith dropped him with a shot from his stungun and jumped over the sprawled body and went sprinting to the skycar. "Sit," he advised Boss Nast, looking in at him from the driver's side.

The lizard raised his dark glasses to get a better look at Smith. "Youse is a dead man," he explained in a grumbly voice.

"I want you to climb, very sedately, out of this crate," instructed Smith, keeping his gun aimed at the fat man.

"Do youse have any idea who you're ordering around, buddy?"

"You sure as hell better be Boss Nast or we wasted the last two hours setting this all up."

"Yeah. I'm Boss Nast and youse are Mr. Dipshit from this moment hence, buddy."

"Out, quick."

The hefty lizardman came grunting out of his bejeweled skycar. "What mob are youse with anyway? Only some jerk with crap for brains would try to—"

"All you have to do, Boss, is tell me where Liz Vertillion is."

"Huh?"

"Lieutenant Vertillion of the Salvation Squad. Where is she?"

The lizard's laugh was a dry, brittle noise. "That nosy bitch? Yeah, she pissed me off, too," he recalled. "But nowhere near as much as youse, buddy."

"I want to find her."

"Don't let me stop youse," Boss Nast said. "Look all youse want, buddy, and when you quit, I'll come and get youse and put your—"

"One is beginning to doubt the efficacy of verbal persuasion and calm reason," put in Saint. Reaching into a pocket, he produced a brand new truthdisc. "What say we avail ourselves of this jolly gimmick I borrowed from the local minions of the law?"

"Might as well."

The lizardman's eyebrows climbed up from behind the protection of his smoky glasses. "Youse guys are really asking for grief if you try to stick that doohickey on me."

"Thing is, Boss," said Smith as he took the metal disc from Saint, "you're not going to be around to do anybody any harm for a while."

"Huh? Listen, buddy, if youse rub me out my mob'll—"

"Nope, we're merely going to transport you to another clime."

"How do you think youse can—"

"They call it telekinesis, old thing."

Whamp!

Smith slapped the disc against Boss Nast's scaly green neck. "Let's get to the questions," he suggested.

20

A breeze came rattling through the artificial jungle. A plaz palm tree at the edge of the pathway Cruz and Jazz were following made a few creaking noises, then toppled over a few yards ahead of them.

"Watch it." Cruz caught the young woman's arm and kept her from progressing.

"I appreciate your concern, Mr. Cruz," she said, pulling free of his grasp. "But even in emergencies I don't relish being handled."

Smiling, Cruz glanced back again over his shoulder. "A reflex action," he said. "Forgive my audacity."

"There's really no need to razz me about what is basically a serious . . . are you still thinking about those jungle women we met at the Main Pavillion?"

Ceasing to look backward, Cruz climbed over the newly fallen tree. "You must admit they were an attractive gaggle of ladies."

"If a bunch of hussies in skimpy animal skin skivvies is your idea of—"

"You weren't as critical of the junglemen."

Scrambling over the imitation tree, Jazz said, "And their dippy names. No wonder nobody much is coming to this con. Camilla, Rulah, Marga, Fantomah . . . dreadful."

"There's the Gorilla House up ahead." Cruz pointed with his metal forefinger.

"Well, Professor Winiarsky's supposed to be living in a hut right behind that," said Jazz. "He must really be in a dire predicament, hiding out here. Gorillas have to be smelly, noisy—"

"They don't keep their paws to themselves either." From his waistband he tugged a small stungun. "Take this, my pet, and go see if the professor's at home. I'll join you shortly."

"At a time like this are you planning on a shabby assignation with one of those jungle bimbos who—"

"Onward," he urged.

The Gorilla House was a large circular building of pale yellow brix, from the inside of which came roars and chest thumpings. Imitation jungle surrounded it.

"I didn't think you could be distracted by the first bare thigh that—"

"I'll be with you soon. Trust me."

Shrugging, Jazz started making her way around the Gorilla House.

After glancing around, Cruz ducked into the wide arched doorway of the big building. He stationed himself close to one wall, covered with shadow, watching the bright day outside.

" . . . Cage Three we see the gorillas spending an idyllic morning in their native habitat," droned the vox-box over the nearest glazfronted display area.

Cruz stroked his metal arm as he waited.

"Bingo," he said to himself a moment later.

Ducked low, he eased out of the building and into the brush.

A slim blonde young woman in a scant costume of black-and-white animal skin had come skulking out of the jungle and was heading for the rear of the place.

Cruz moved silently after her.

When he was a few feet behind her, he said, "Halt if you please, Camilla. So we can have a chat about why you're following us."

She spun, reaching toward the dagger at her slim waist.

Cruz said, "I want to talk, but I don't want you to conk out the way the last alfie did. So I—"

"What did you call me?" Her hand closed around the hilt of the knife.

"So I'm hoping you don't go blooey if I just hypnotize you." He held up his metal palm toward her. "We'll give it a try. Concentrate now, Camilla, on the whirling circle you see in my hand. . . ."

Saint gave his white tunic an annoyed tug. "Off-the-rack garments never fit one as well as tailormade," he remarked as they rode the ramp toward the entrance to the Tech Hill Mental Health Centre.

"We didn't exactly have time to visit a tailor," reminded Smith, who was also clad in a two-piece white medisuit.

Tech Hill was a complex of five large domed buildings, surrounded by grassy fields and woodlands.

"Actually my favorite tailor is in the Earth System." The green man smoothed the front of his doctor tunic. "On the Planet Earth in a city called Hong Kong. Incredibly gifted chap, who knows exactly how to compensate for a very minute difference in the height of my manly shoulders."

At the top of the ramp stood a tall nightguard robot, his coppery body rich with tiny bulbs of light. "ID packets," he croaked, scannerhand extending.

"I am Mind Doctor Lowenkopf," announced Saint grandly, "and this is my noted colleague, Doctor Matcha."

"Talk is cheap. Let's see some ID, gents." The two rows of little lights ringing the robot's broad chest were changing from yellow to crimson.

"Yes, to be sure." Saint drew a packet of identification materials out of his breast pocket and deposited them on the mechanical guard's palm.

From deep inside the robot came a faint clucking as the scanner built into his hand went over the packet. "All in order, you may enter."

Smith's papers produced a similar reaction.

Inside the first dome of Tech Hill Saint went striding over to the reception desk. "I am Mind Doctor Lowenkopf," he told the camera eye floating above the desk, "and I have here a Release Order for Patient PR/104."

"So let's see it, buster."

"Here you are." With a flourish and a bow Saint placed a sheet of crisp lavender sewdopape on the exact center of the glaz desk.

"All in order. Continue to Dome 3, Level B."

"Thank you so much."

When they were riding the moving ramp to the Third Dome, Smith said, "You did a nifty job of getting us the right papers and altering them to fit."

"A mere bagatelle, old chap, for one with my telek abilities." Smith tugged at the hem of his white tunic. "I must remember to teleport the real Lowenkopf and Matcha back from that remote stretch of the Red Desert I sent them to once we wrap up this phase of things."

Smith said, "I just hope there's something left of Liz Vertillion."

"Tech Hills is a very posh institution. They treat their

inmates well," said Saint. "Boss Nast could've dumped your old schoolmate in a far worse spot."

"That bastard. 'The more I don't like 'em, the more I want they should suffer.' " Smith shook his head. "Casual enemies he just kills, someone like Liz he rail-roads into this joint under a fake name. Jobs all the papers to make it look like she's hopelessly insane."

"A timehonored method of taking care of one's rivals and enemies, old boy."

"That doesn't make—"

"Pay attention to me!" A small middle-aged man, wearing only a short neowool robe, came running out of a room on their left. He hopped on the ramp, catching hold of Smith's hand. "Pay attention to me! Nobody in this damn hole is at all interested in my troubles or—"

"Myron, Myron." Two childsize robots scooted out of the room, hit the ramp and ran along it until they caught up with the unhappy man in the robe. "We care."

"See?" said Myron, squeezing at Smith's hand with both of his. "A couple of clunky machines who talk in unison. Is that affection? Is that supportive concern for—"

"Myron, Myron. We like you, we support your every activity." Both tackled him, one high and the other low. "We dote on you, in fact. C'mon back to your nice room. Okay?"

"It's not nice. It's bleak, heartless . . ."

Twin tranquilizer shots, delivered by the needleguns built into the right hands of each nursebot, put Myron to sleep.

"Excuse us." The two little robots hefted the sleeping Myron off the ramp and onto a sidestrip. "You know how it is with somebody who's goofy."

"Perfectly understandable," said Saint.

•   •   •

"I just knew it." Jazz gave a disappointed shake of her head. "Can't you leave your stupefied lady friend conquests elsewhere when you come paying social—"

"Hush, my pet." He carried Camilla all the way into the reed hut. "I want Winiarsky to hear this."

The runaway professor was a tall, lank man in his early thirties, bearded. "Are you this Cruz that Jazzmin has been telling me about?"

"The same." He deposited the body of the hypnotized alfie on a cot that sat on a very believable groutskin rug. "She's not rigged to destruct if questioned this way, proving the opposition doesn't think of everything."

"You mean she isn't just looped from the booze you were probably guzzling off in the bushes?" asked the still indignant Jazz.

Ignoring her entirely, Cruz knelt beside the cot. "Camilla, tell me again who you work for."

"That should be whom," muttered the professor.

"I'm on special assignment for the Covert Public Relations Department of Syndek," she said in a low even voice, eyes remaining tight shut.

"Why are you here posing as a jungleperson?"

"Mr. Bjorn assigned me," she replied.

"Who's Bjorn?"

"The Chief Troubleshooter."

"Not an alfie?"

"No, he's a real person. Humanoid."

"Continue."

"Mr. Bjorn had received an unconfirmed report that you two, Cruz and the reporter, might be coming to Jungleland. That tied in with earlier intelligence that Winiarsky had been spotted in the area."

"What do you do when you find Winiarsky?"

"Capture him."

"And then?"

"He is to be incapacitated and delivered to Mr. Bjorn."

"Where?"

"I am to contact Mr. Bjorn and he'll inform me where to drop Winiarsky."

Standing up and back, Cruz stroked his moustache. "I think mayhap I'll have the lass drop me on Bjorn instead," he said thoughtfully. "That'll no doubt lead to lively times for all concern—"

"You can't do that," cried Jazz. "They'll kill—"

"Say, wait a moment," put in the professor. "Are you implying that if I were turned over to this Bjorn fellow I, too, would be killed? I wasn't aware, when I decided to hide out, that my plight was quite that—"

"That's what I've been trying to tell you while I thought he was off cavorting," she said, twisting her fingers together. "All sorts of people are hunting you, some with rather base motives."

"Jazz," said Cruz, "I'll fix it so you can take Winiarsky to the safe hideout where we've got Ruiz stashed."

"Would that be Oscar Ruiz? He and I grew up together at Horizon—"

"Which is what's behind this whole delightful escapade," said Cruz. "Listen attentively and I'll give you a concise rundown. Then we'll get you safely clear and I'll set up a rendezvous with the Bjorn gent."

She was a thin darkhaired young woman, her cheekbones prominent, her large eyes underscored with shadows. "Now what?" she said in a faraway voice when Smith and Saint entered her room.

"Liz?" Smith looked at the young woman sitting up on the floating bed, unsure he had the right patient.

She studied him for a moment. "I don't see the purpose of this," she said finally. "Getting someone to look like Jared Smith. How can that hurt me any more than the—"

"I am Jared," he assured her, crossing to the bed. This was Liz Vertillion, but much changed.

"I don't think I believe that," she said. "I don't believe anything, haven't for a long time."

"Dear lady." Saint perched on the edge of the narrow bed. "You can believe in us. We've come here, at considerable risk, to spring you from this vile—"

"Oh." Liz put her thin hand up to her mouth, rolled her eyes at the ceiling. "If that's true, you've screwed it up by saying so right out loud. They watch and listen to everything I do and say in here and now they—"

"We fixed that before dropping in," explained Smith, taking her arm. "But in ten minutes or so one of their security mechs may start getting uneasy. Which is why you'd better gather your stuff and—"

"I don't have anything, Jared. Only this hospital gown."

"Fear not, dear lady." Saint reached into an inner pocket of his tunic to produce a small parcel. "This spoiled the line of my outfit, but it couldn't be helped. You'll find a lightweight allpurpose shift folded neatly within. Not the most stylish of garments, yet—"

"Is he a conman, Jared?"

"Not at the moment, though usually."

"Funny. I guessed he was, but I believe him."

Saint said, "You are a deucedly perceptive wench."

"Jared?" With his help she left the bed. "Is it all right if I don't understand what's going on?"

"Yep, don't worry about that." He put an arm around her narrow shoulders.

21

Cruz landed the skycar in the quiet jungle clearing. "Heckling will do you not a shred of good, my pet," he told Jazz.

"You're really being incredibly stupid." She was in the passenger seat beside him, slouched, arms folded. "Putting yourself into the jaws of Syndek is—"

"Jazzmin," put in Winiarsky from the back seat, "as a neutral observer, allow me to point out that—"

"But you aren't a neutral in this," she said impatiently. "Syndek wants you, too. They want to pump your brain dry, then dump you someplace."

"Even so, what I hear from my vantage point is—"

"Oh, calamity! Quit lecturing me, since I'm no longer—"

"We all get out here," mentioned Cruz as he dropped from the cab to the orange moss of the clearing.

Coming toward them from the neolog hunting lodge some fifty yards distant was a large jungle-green robot.

"Ah, it is Bwana Cruz unless these eyes fool me."

"I think your boss is expecting me, Tomo."

"He is, most anxiously. For we have a saying here in the Great Jungle . . ." Tomo paused, raising a metal finger to his metal chin. "But, alas, it appears to have been erased from my store of useful aphorisms. Pity."

A small, wiry man with shortcropped greying hair stepped out onto the shady verandah of the lodge. He wore a two-piece tan huntsuit. "Glad I could be of help," he said as he came down the steps.

"If you really want to help, Mr. Macumazahn," said Jazz, who'd disembarked and was standing close to Cruz, "you'll convince him to drop his crackpot scheme."

"This is Jazz Miller," introduced Cruz. "And Professor Winiarsky."

Tomo was peering into the skycar, chuckling. "Running true to form, Bwana Cruz," he said. "Bringing along not one but two pretty ladies. This one in here, though, seems to be out cold."

"I'd be grateful if you toted her inside, Tomo."

"Glad to oblige, sir."

Henry Macumazahn said, "Right after you called, Cruz, I had Tomo run my spare skyvan out of the hangar. It's beyond the house, ready to take off."

"We have a saying about gratitude, Henry, but it slips my mind." Smiling, he glanced skyward. "Nobody tagged us from Jungleland, but I think it's best that Jazz and the professor make the rest of their trip in another craft. That way—"

"Fooey," said the reporter. "I'm not budging. Because if you honestly think I'm going to let you commit suicide, Mr. Cruz, you—"

"Young woman," said Macumazahn. "Take the advice of a fellow who's led many an expedition in dangerous country. There can be only one leader and if—"

"Who voted him boss?" She jerked a thumb, angry, at Cruz. "I volunteered to tag along, but that doesn't include standing back while—"

"You don't seem to have much faith in him," said the hunter. "I myself am certain Cruz will come out on top."

"This is not an actual authentic female," mentioned Tomo, who was carrying the unconscious Camilla toward the house.

"Merely a reasonable facsimile," said Cruz. "Now, Jazz, I have to see about putting through the pixphone call to Bjorn. You and the professor head on to the Museum."

Dust swirled up when she stomped her foot. "Why don't we all go? Then you and Mr. Smith and that polite Mr. Saint can all sit around and discuss—"

"We're beyond sitting around," Cruz told her.

"He's absolutely right," said Winiarsky. "We'd better get moving, Jazzmin."

She hesitated, taking a slow deep breath. "Okay, I won't let the team down," she said finally. "But I still am convinced you're being dippy."

"Skinny is a better word," said Liz Vertillion.

"On the contrary, my dear, a deucedly more appropriate one is slender." Saint was looking back at her over the top of the passenger seat of their skycar.

Huddled on the backseat, wearing the simple dress he'd brought, Liz said, "You really are a conman, aren't you?"

"That doesn't mean one's lost the ability to speak the

truth," the green man assured her. "Despite your ordeal, you are still a most attractive young woman."

"A most attractive *skinny* young woman," she said, smiling faintly. "Jared, I feel somewhat less fuzzy-headed now. Maybe you could try to explain what's going on."

Smith was piloting the skycar across the night city. "We found out from Boss Nast where you'd gotten to," he said. "Then we—"

"Backtrack a moment," Liz requested. "How the heck'd you manage to get him to talk to you at all?"

"Saint and I make a very persuasive combination."

"In addition to my many manifest gifts, I'm also an excellent telek."

"I helped rehabilitate a couple of them at the Mission."

"I'm not quite ready for salvation, my dear."

"Jared, it's been years since we've seen each . . . although once, some months ago, I saw a hopeless derelict stumbling through our district. He looked something like you and I tried to follow. But I lost him in the fog and—"

"Probably was me," he said. "I'm just getting over a protracted bout of self-pity."

"Still because of Jennifer?"

"Thought I was long cured, but then she married. . . ." He shrugged.

Reaching out, Liz touched his shoulder. "I was going to ask why you came looking for me at all. Not that I don't sure as heck appreciate it."

"Originally I was hired, as was Saint here, to track down five missing Horizon House kids," he answered. "We were told that Jennifer and her mother wanted to have a reunion and were anxious to find every kid who was still alive."

"Aren't we all still alive?"

"Nope, but I'll get to that shortly," said Smith.

"The first point to grasp, Elizabeth," said Saint, "is that our employer, the illustrious Whistler Agency, was not entirely candid and open with us. They maintain, by way of mitigation, that their client, Triplan, Ltd., was most stingy with the truth."

"That's the outfit Jennifer's husband is associated with, isn't it?"

"The same," said Smith. "Turns out Doctor Westerland picked ten of us, you and me included, Liz, for a special sort of mission in life."

"What are you talking about? I don't remember anything like that."

"Exactly." Smith went on and explained things to her.

When he concluded, Liz said, "I'm disappointed. In Doctor Westerland, I mean. To use us like that and not even—"

"He was killed, remember, before he could do much of anything about—"

"Jared, you don't believe he ever would've told us, do you?"

"I guess not, no."

Liz said, "Are you taking me back to the Mission or do you still intend to turn me over to—"

"I intend to try and save our lives."

"Remember, my dear," added Saint, "that, as Smith told you, the Syndek operatives are not above killing you Horizon alumni once they've siphoned off what you know."

She folded her hands. "Poor Hal Larzon."

"What I want to do is get you to a safe hideaway," Smith said, frowning at the control dash. "Oscar Ruiz is already there, Winiarsky should be soon. We're in a position to make a deal with Triplan, since we've been used as carriers for this information without ever being asked about it.''

"I'm not sure I exactly want compensation, although I don't fancy being hunted. And I suppose with money I could help the Mission to accomplish a lot of . . . what's wrong, Jared?"

"The controls seem to have locked on me," he said as he struggled with the drivestick and pushed at the buttons on the dash. "Saint, can you—"

"I've been trying to use my telek powers on them for the past couple of minutes, old boy," he said. "Having, I fear, deuced bad luck thus far."

"Shit, somebody's planted a parasite controlbox under our car." Smith kept trying to regain control of the skycar. "We're being flown to somebody else's destination."

22

"Jove, one is sorry this wasn't mentioned earlier."

"You certain you can't?"

Saint, face dotted with perspiration, nodded abjectly. "I'm not affected by being up in this skycar, old man, yet to go outside there and crawl under the ship . . ."

"Okay, can't be helped." Smith snatched the small toolkit off the cabin wall. "I'll swing down there and—"

"Why can't Saint use his telek gift to get rid of that parasite control gadget?" Liz asked.

"Alas, I can't teleport anything I haven't first seen," he explained forlornly. "And severe vertigo makes it impossible, even in this desperate instance, for one to—"

"Take the driveseat," Smith told him, moving to the door. "When I get rid of the damn box, be ready to get us back on our own course."

"Yes, to be sure."

The skycar was flying south, heading for the edge of the night city.

"Be careful," said Liz.

"Intend to." Even though he opened the door carefully, the rush of air outside yanked the handle from his grasp.

Giving an annoyed shake of his head, Smith stepped out onto the wing. He had the small toolkit tucked into his waistband.

The wind pushed and tugged at him. He took one wobbly step, unexpectedly sat down, and slid toward the car wing's front edge.

His legs shot out into the darkness beyond.

Smith twisted his body, catching the edge of the wing as he fell by.

As he dangled there the wind did an even more enthusiastic job of shoving at him.

He inched closer to the body of the skycar. Then he stretched, and grabbed at the rigid landing gear.

Smith managed to catch hold just above a fender and brought his other hand over. Now he was hanging beneath the belly of the flying machine.

Down below the city was ending, few lights showed and they seemed to be flying over forest country.

Smith took a few slow, deep breaths before swinging his legs up and locking them around the axle. Turning and twisting, he pulled himself up and inched out until he was sitting, hunched, on the thing.

The skycar seemed to be losing altitude now that it had left the city behind.

From the kit Smith extracted a small palmlight. Clicking it on, he swept the underside of the machine with a thin beam of light.

"C'mon, c'mon," he said aloud. "Where are you?"

He didn't spot the coinsized parasite control box until he made his second sweep. The little gadget was attached to the fuselage above the other wheel.

Smith bumped his backside along the axle until he was directly under the damn thing.

The car was whizzing along just above the treetops.

Smith played the light on the box. Since it was a magnetic model, all he had to do was . . .

Glancing down, he saw a rectangle of light rushing toward them.

A landing field, lit by two long rows of ground spots. A domed barn at the far side of the field. And standing in front of that barn, smiling up into the night, was Deac Constiner of the Trinidad Law Bureau.

Smith caught hold of the parasite, tugging at it. For a few seconds it wouldn't budge. Then it came free in his hand.

He teetered on the axle, regained his balance, tossed the gadget away.

"Take us up!" he shouted.

Constiner ducked to his left as the parasite came whistling down at him.

The skycar started climbing, up and away from the field and the waiting lawman.

"Now," said Smith, "let's see if I can get myself back inside."

Cruz gritted his teeth a moment after he'd turned off the highway onto the sideroad leading to Pastoral Estates. The road was rutted and cracked, causing his newly acquired landvan to bounce and rattle.

The giant plaz cockroach atop the roof creaked, shimmied.

On each side of the pale green vehicle were the words *Sonic Bros., Bugkillers Deluxe* in glowing twists of neon.

As Cruz drove through the rusted weedy gateway of the decaying housing development a shaggy goat broke free of the cluster of green nomads camped on the nearest overgrown lawn. It ran, bleeting, almost into the path of his landvan. Swerving, Cruz nearly drove up onto the opposite curve.

That action scattered the small band of looters, mostly ragged catmen, who were carrying off the shutters and patio brix from another of the forlorn houses.

Getting himself back on course, Cruz drove along Sylvan Lane to Shady Glen and turned left.

Halfway up the next block a dumpy lizardwoman in a polkadot housecoat leaped in front of his landvan.

Cruz whapped the brake button. The van shuddered, and stopped about four feet short of smacking her. The giant cockroach made a protesting noise.

After activating the window-lowering toggle, Cruz put his head out into the gathering darkness. "What is the meaning of this rash act, madam?"

She held her thumb an inch and a half from her forefinger. "About this long," she said, shuffling around to his side of the cab. "A disgusting scummy shade of brown. Stunted little wings and a bunch of teenie weenie googly eyes. What is it?"

"You nearly get yourself plowed under just to ask me riddles?"

"Whatever it is . . . I got me ten thousand of the rascals crawling all over my kitchen," she explained. "We're one of the few decent families left in this sinkhole of a community. Now, as if we didn't have enough to bear with nomads barbecuing goats on our lawns and looters and mewts and welfs and . . . now we've been cursed with a blight of disgusting slimy brown things. Oh, and they eat linoleum.''

"I happen to be enroute to a home with an even more momentous problem.'' Cruz reached behind him. "However, spray this on the beggars and it'll work wonders until I can get back to you.'' He grabbed up a spraygun, tossed it out into the oncoming night to her.

"Bless you, sir . . . wait now! This says BriteKoat Wallpaint/Lemon Brickle Shade #2. How in Plaut's name can paint—''

"Trust me. This is, after all, my profession.'' He rolled up the window, released the brake and rolled on.

Two blocks farther on he spotted the Pastoral Estates Middle School. Cruz drove on by the weedfilled playground and the ramshackle buildings to park a block away.

As he stepped from the landvan a pudgy humanoid boy of ten popped up on the other side of a dying hedge.

"Better pay me ten trubux to watch your car, chump,'' he advised. "Otherwise severe damage and looting is likely to—''

"Ah, I never worry about things like that,'' Cruz informed him. "This thing's equipped with Kilguard.''

"Kilguard? What the heck's that?''

"Just touch one dainty finger to this vehicle and you'll get the answer to that question, my lad.'' Smiling, Cruz went off.

When darkness filled the schoolgrounds, Cruz moved clear of the overgrown shubbery at their edge to go sprinting over to the nearest building. Getting inside was simple, since the door had long ago been taken away.

Moving around the remains of a nomad cookfire, he eased along the dark hallway.

Bjorn, contacted on the pixphone by the mind-controlled Camilla, had told the imitation junglegirl to come to this abandoned school complex at nine tonight and leave the stunned body of Professor Winiarsky in the pantry of the cafeteria.

Cruz stationed himself in a closet that gave him a view of the only entrances to the cafeteria. It was a few minutes past eight.

There were a radio and a tiny earphone built into his metal arm. Cruz, hunkered in the closet, tried to find a newscast but couldn't bring in anything but a local music station that was featuring three hours of uninterrupted music by the Sophisticates.

He waited patiently in silence.

Eleven minutes shy of nine Cruz heard footfalls.

Two people approached the cafeteria.

" . . . like little old aunties," a harsh croaking voice was complaining. "We ought to quit behaving that way and get tough."

"That's not Syndek policy, Otto."

"Which is exactly why, Mr. Bjorn, if you don't mind my saying, we're not getting anyplace in this blasted quest."

The two men halted a few feet from Cruz' hiding place.

"We'll finally have one of the Horizon Kids in a few minutes now," said Bjorn. He was a tall man with white hair; his companion was a thickset toadman. "And all we need, Otto, is one part of the Westerland secret and we can bargain with Triplan and whoever else is interested."

"That's fine, but I still don't see why we have to keep this guy alive after we—"

"Syndek does business in certain ways. No killing. Ever."

"Stupid damn way to—"

"Quiet down now, Otto. We'll go inside to await our delivery."

Cruz was rubbing his metal thumb knuckle across his moustache. "That wasn't a faked conversation," he told himself. "They didn't have any notion I was lurking nearby."

If that were true, it meant Syndek agents hadn't been the ones who'd gotten to Hal Larzon and killed him.

"Who then?" Cruz asked himself as he slipped silently out of his hiding place.

23 ═══════════════════════

The airfloat train rushed through the sunbright afternoon fields. There were rolling hills, rich with high orange grass, a few farmhouses with sharply slanting sewdoshingle roofs. Far off, in the hazy distance, a herd of grazing grouts.

Smith watched the familiar countryside unwind beyond the windows of his compartment. Just about everything seemed to be the same as it had been when he was growing up in this territory years ago. He felt neither depressed nor elated about being here again.

When the train began moving through shadowy woodlands, Smith stood and lifted his small suitcase from under the seat.

"Crosscut Station," crackled the voxbox in the compartment ceiling.

The train slowed, shuddered slightly, came to a stop.

The platformside door opened with a shushing sound and Smith stepped from the train.

Standing over near the small, sewdoshingle station

house, shielded by a striped sunbrella and wearing a three-piece checkered knickersuit, was Saint. Tipping his checkered cap, he came strolling over. "One supposes this is a bit of a sentimental journey, eh?"

Shrugging, Smith followed the green man over to an open landcar. "I haven't burst into tears yet."

Saint folded up his umbrella and mounted the driveseat. "It's the things that happen inside one do most of the damage," he observed. "I take it, old man, you escorted the charming Miss Vertillion to safety at the Robotics Museum hideaway."

"She's there, along with Ruiz and Winiarsky." He took the passenger seat. "So's Jazz Miller, complaining about not being at the forefront of things. It seems Cruz—"

"You'll find Cruz at the cozy countryhouse I've rented." Saint started the vehicle.

"How'd he—"

"Cruz pixed the satellite, learned from the estimable Jazz that you were enroute to the idyllic scenes of your youth and popped over. He's come up with some interesting, though perplexing, scraps of intelligence."

"Such as?"

"I'd rather he tell you."

Smith watched the fields and hills they were driving through. "See that ruined temple up there?"

"A very picturesque pile."

"That was one of the places where Jennifer and I used to meet," said Smith. "The place is about five miles from Horizon House, which is on the other side of that hill."

"In the brief time I've been a resident I've managed to visit a few of the local inns and pubs," said Saint. "At a quaint establishment called the Snerg & Racket I encountered a fetching, though fleshy, barmaid who spoke quite highly of you."

"What the hell brought me up as a topic?"

"Someone mentioned Jennifer Westerland Arloff and your name came up as a result," replied Saint, drumming his fingers lightly on the steering wheel as he guided the landcar through the afternoon. "One gathers you were somewhat more charming then than you are at present."

"Why was Jennifer being discussed?"

"The lady has returned to her ancestral home, supposedly to participate in a fundraising fete to be held at Horizon House tomorrow."

Smith had been watching three pale yellow gulls circling high overhead. "But actually she must've come back to question Annalee Kitchen."

"That was my conclusion, yes, old man."

"What about Arloff?"

"He remains in the capital."

Smith said, "I don't want to run into Jennifer as yet."

"You've little reason to fear that. Our domicile is rather secluded."

"Can anybody attend these upcoming festivities at Horizon House?"

"Yes, which will afford me an excellent excuse for poking about the premises," said Saint. "I intend to pay my five trubux entry bright and early on the morrow."

"You ought to be able to find out most of what we still want to know at Horizon House," said Smith. "I'll whip you up a hand-drawn map of the places you better get a look at."

"One is confident that tomorrow shall prove fruitful." Saint turned onto a treelined side road.

A half-mile farther along he slowed to drive on through the open gateway in a high wall of faded yellow brix. A brass plate on the righthand gatepost announced that the name of the estate was *Tranquil Acres*.

"Tranquil Acres?" said Smith.

"We're only renting," reminded Saint.

Cruz had removed his mechanical arm and had it sitting on the top of the big neowood desk in the large den of their countryhouse. Small tools were scattered around on the plyoblotter. He was seated behind the desk, an electropik in his left hand, tinkering with the arm. Out beyond the windows behind him stretched an acre of closecropped yellow grass that eased down to a wide pond. Three pale lavender swans were drifting by.

"You're right," Smith said as he paced in front of the empty fireplace. "What you've told us does cause me to have some second thoughts about this whole damn mess."

"It's good for the system, old chum," said Cruz, "to find out some of your assumptions were cockeyed."

Saint was on a loveseat, an album of tri-op photos open upon his lap. "One doesn't doubt your thoroughness, Cruz," he said, "yet it's deuced difficult to believe that—"

"I didn't rely on what I overheard Bjorn and his henchman saying," Cruz reiterated. "No, I snuck up on the lads, stunned them both and used a truthdisc on each in turn." He tapped his metal wrist with the tool he was using. "Syndek did not kill Hal Larzon, and they don't have the information he was carrying around. Someone else entirely laid the unfortunate fellow low. Winiarsky was to be their first captured Horizon Kid."

Smith asked, "Does Bjorn have any notions as to who did get to Larzon?"

"He suspects a representative of the Whistler Agency,

or mayhap one of the Triplan ops."

"The Triplan chaps," pointed out Saint as he absently turned a page in the album, "would have no reason to resort to murder."

"And nobody at Syndek knows the trigger word," asked Smith, "knows how to get the carriers to talk?"

"No, Bjorn was going to depend on electronic means to get at what Westerland hid away long ago." Cruz gave his arm a slow scrutiny before reattaching it to his flesh elbow.

"How'd they know about the damn secret at all?"

"The information was sold to them, for the handsome fee of four hundred thousand trubux," answered Cruz while flexing his metal fingers. "All this was set up by way of blanked pixphone screens, scrambled voices, neutral computer terminals. Bjorn doesn't know, although they were slipped enough information to convince them there really is a valuable secret to be had, who his contact is."

"Jove, it must be someone within Triplan then."

"Or someone at Horizon House." Smith sat on the edge of a fat purple armchair.

"Our rivals at Syndek are all at sea it would seem, but do either of you chaps have the foggiest notion who dispatched the Larzon bloke?" asked Saint.

Cruz said, "Jared, you know Deac Constiner better than we do. Could he—"

"Nope, not Constiner." Smith shook his head. "He doesn't work that way. If he'd found Hal Larzon he'd simply have taken him into a TLB station."

"Then we have to assume," said Saint, "that we've got competition we don't even know about."

"Maybe," said Smith.

24

A lizardman on a bicycle went rattling by Saint on the morning road, splashing dust on him. "Sorry, gov," called the lizard, taking a hand off the handlebars to tip his strawhat.

"Think nothing of it, old chap." Tugging out a plyo-chief, Saint brushed at his face and then the front of his three-piece cazsuit. He smiled, continuing to act the part of an amiable tourist.

The Horizon House grounds covered twenty acres and were fenced in by high hedges and stretches of woodland. The main entrance was usually guarded by a massive black wrought iron gate, but that had been thrown open wide this morning. Seated on either side of the gate, at folding plaz tables, were humanoid ladies in flowered dresses and widebrimmed hats. At least a dozen customers for the charity fete were lined up at each table to purchase tickets.

"My, ain't it grand," remarked the catwoman Saint took a place behind. "All them lovely towers and all."

"Have you never seen Horizon House before, Madam?"

Shaking her furry head, she replied, "Not so much as a squint, sir. I live over in the next territory and I've not visited hereabouts before."

The house was imposing, a complex of towers and wings, built of pale rose brix and topped with slanting neotile roofs. There was much wrought iron, considerable clinging ivy of a faded seablue shade. There were many striped tents and multicolored stands set up on the vast lawns, along with a merry-go-round, complete with calliope, and a makeshift track for field events. On a floating dais near the main entrance of the house a string quartet, consisting of two tuxsuited toadmen, a humanoid blonde woman in a sequinsuit and a catman draped in an opera cloak, was tuning up.

"Five trudollars is a bit dear," observed the catwoman as she bought her ticket. "But the day'll be well worth it, I fancy."

"And the money, dear lady, goes to a good cause." Although Saint had forgotten exactly what charity was to benefit, he assumed it must be a worthwhile one.

"Yes, that's certainly true." She rubbed her paws together. "Well, me for the jumble sale. And you, sir?"

"I shall stroll about for a bit." Giving her a slight bow, he moved off along a pathway paved with yellow gravel.

Three small catgirls, each in a crisp pink frock, came running at him across the grass. "Please, sir," said one meekly, "where do you suppose the Children's Mixed Chorus has gotten to?"

Saint leaned down closer to the trio. "Would you little ladies be strayed members of that organization?"

"Yes, and we're supposed to start singing right now and it's not in the tent where we rehearsed yesterday or the day before either."

Straightening, Saint took a careful look around the front acres. "I fancy I see what looks to be the makings of a mixed chorus flocking into that orange-and-blue tent up yonder."

"Where, where?" The fuzzy little singer stretched up on tiptoe.

Saint lifted her up to his shoulder. "Next to the lemonade stand, do you see?"

"Oh, yes, and that's Mrs. Dubay, the Assistant Leader, standing out in front of the tent and looking like she doesn't know where to set that plate of watercress sandwiches someone's handed her."

Lowering the little catgirl to the grass, Saint said, "You're no longer lost, ladies."

"Thank you, sir."

He strolled on.

The calliope was slightly off key, but the merry-go-round was a handsome thing. There were gilded neo-wood horses, grouts, giant snergs, wolos, unicorns, bears.

"Jove, that must be the woman in the case," Saint told himself, slowing.

Coming down the brix steps of Horizon House was a young woman who was, judging by photos he'd seen, Jennifer Westerland Arloff. She wore a simple suitdress and did not appear to be especially happy.

Saint paused at a display of homebaked pies and cakes, still watching Jennifer as she made her way onto the grounds. "Not a bad looking creature, although on the slender side," he decided. "Yet hardly the type, one would think, to drive a man to ruin and despair. Yet she did just that to Smith . . . or rather Smith did that to Smith and blamed this young lady. Seriously doubt she'd have that effect on me, though, of course, I'm a bit more hardhearted than is Smith."

". . . hooglyberries," the plumpish lizardwoman

behind the bake table was saying to him.

"Beg pardon?"

"The pie you're admiring is made from fresh hoogly-berries."

"Ah, indeed? One's mouth commences watering," he informed her. "Ere I depart, I'll purchase it."

"Best do it now, since hooglyberry pies sell exceptionally well."

"Reluctantly I must take my chances, since I don't wish to be burdened with it as yet."

"I could put it aside, sir, with your name on—"

"What you could do for me, my dear," confided Smith, "is answer a rather personal question."

She blinked. "Well, I suppose if it's—"

"Can you tell me where to find the restrooms?"

She pointed toward the big house. "They've been set up on the north side of the mansion."

"Thank you so much." He smiled, bowed and moved on.

On the north side of the house, according to the map Smith had drawn for him, there was an entry to a part of the house Saint very much wanted to see.

Saint paused in the silent shadowy hallway to admire the thick patterned carpeting he was tredding on. "Quite charming," he murmured.

From his breast pocket he took Smith's drawing of the Horizon House floorplan for this section of the sprawling mansion. The first room he wanted to get a look at ought to be just around the next turning.

"Oh, I say, this will never do," said a thin, rattling voice behind him. "No, no, dear me, not at all."

Executing a slow about face, the green man found himself confronting a large chromeplated robot butler "Were you addressing me, my man?"

"These fetes, these fetes. Such low types come flocking," sighed the butler. "And when one of them actually intrudes upon—"

"There appears to be some misunderstanding," said Saint with a smile. "I happen to be, and I'm rather puzzled at your not recognizing me, Beemis, Count Japhet Seagate. I am a longtime chum of dear old Mrs. Westerland and—"

"No, you aren't. You're nothing more nor less than a seedy gatecrasher, no doubt intent on making off with the plates after tracking up the runners."

Saint gave a resigned little smile. "Well, you've certainly seen through me."

"Now then, march your squatty form out of here at once," ordered Beemis. "Or I'll be forced to . . . um . . . that's . . . odd . . ."

"Eh?"

"I seem to be . . . yes . . . having . . . trouble remembering . . ."

"Don't fret about that, old thing," advised Saint. "I'm simply using my telek powers to diddle with your brain. The idea being that you'll forget all about my visit."

"You . . . shan't . . ."

"It's not difficult at all to manipulate the components of your thinking system," Saint explained. "You'll remember my hasty visit not at all. And you'll remain here, glued to the spot as it were, with that barmy expression on your moon face for exactly one-half hour. Understand?"

"Yes . . . understand . . ."

Saint resumed his prowl.

25

"You ought to cultivate the ability to relax," suggested Cruz, who was reclining in a wicker armchair in the shady arbor at the rear of their countryhouse.

Smith was pacing the grass, twisting a short length of vine between his fingers. "Saint's overdue," he said.

"No doubt he dallied to kiss a few hands. These charity bazaars draw exactly the sort of well-to-do matrons among whom he shines. No need to—"

"Here he comes."

The green man was sauntering toward them from the direction of the house. "One sincerely hopes one hasn't kept all and sundry waiting," he said. "I paused within to shower and change."

"Did you get into Horizon House?"

Saint, who was wearing a two-piece off-white lounge-suit, arranged himself on a neowood bench and, carefully, crossed his legs. "All went according to plan," he answered. "I had a peek at Mrs. Westerland's parlor,

Jennifer's study and both the Horizon House computer rooms. I had to temporarily incapacitate one robot butler, two robot guards and an android housemaid who was actually named Fifi. None, of course, will recall my brief intrusion.''

"So now you can, since you've had a look at the layouts, teleport anything that's in—"

"By the bye, I caught a glimpse of Jennifer," added Saint. "She's looking rather wan and—"

"Mrs. Westerland's files first," Smith told him.

Nodding, Saint locked his hands over one knee and shut his eyes. "Won't take a moment," he promised.

There was a faint popping, then a thin plazcovered folder materialized on the bench beside him.

"Better allow me to peruse it first," offered Cruz, reaching over to pick it up. "In case it contains the triggering phrase, Jared. Just looking at it might cause you to pop into a trance state."

"Go ahead."

Cruz settled back into his chair, leafed through the several sheets of faxpape. "Only one item of interest herein," he announced finally. "Triplan, Ltd. is actually owned by Mrs. Westerland, Jennifer Arloff and her husband. Seems the late Doctor Westerland formed this company on the sly some years ago." He closed the folder, passed it over to Smith.

Taking it, Smith told Saint, "See what you can find in Jennifer's study."

"Yes, I know exactly what's wanted from therein." Concentrating again, he produced a plazcovered book.

Cruz checked through that first. Finishing, he coughed into his metal fist. "These are safe for you to scan, Jared," he said. "They do, however, present us with a source of perplexity."

"How so?"

"These are Jennifer's confidential memos to herself on the recent phases of the quest for her father's lost secret." Cruz tapped the book against his thigh. "According to these only three people know about the secret in all its aspects. That's Jennifer, her mother and Arloff."

"Jove, then one of the three has to be the person who's doublecrossing Triplan," said Saint, "selling tips to Syndek and sending Larzon on to glory, eh."

"We got hold of this information," Smith reminded him. "That means someone else could've, too."

"It wasn't anyone from Syndek," said Cruz. "I confirmed that with Bjorn. They haven't as yet tapped any Triplan or Horizon House sources of information."

Saint said, "I can't swear to this, yet I'm near certain no one except myself has been probing Triplan or Horizon House."

"How do you know that?"

He rubbed at his curly orange hair. "One can sense that sort of thing, old man. Obviously I'm not completely certain, since it's a feeling rather than—"

"Okay, let's say you're right," said Smith. "Why would any of these people doublecross the others?"

"Money's always a good motive," mentioned Cruz.

"Meaning that if one of them got the secret all to himself, there wouldn't be any splitting of profits."

"And Syndek could probably be blamed."

"I'd hazard a guess," said Saint, "that Arloff is the most likely candidate. I find it difficult to accept your Jennifer betraying her own mother."

"She's not my Jennifer, but I agree. She and her parents were very close, loyal and—"

"I wouldn't rule anyone out," put in Cruz.

"Even so," said Smith, "I'd better arrange to meet with Jennifer. We have to talk."

Cruz eyed him for a few silent seconds. "You still haven't gotten over—"

"If her husband's working against her, I have to mention that fact to her, Cruz."

"She won't believe you, old chum. I've known a lot of other men's wives in my time and this seems like—"

"Now get me whatever the computers have on Annalee Kitchen," Smith told the green man.

"Yes, have that in a jiffy." He closed his eyes tight. A moment later several sheets of yellow faxpape were in his hands. Saint glanced through the material. "Yes, this is an account of the extracting of the portion of the secret that the Kitchen woman carried in her head. The information itself is also here, along with the triggering phrase. Which phrase is a sequence of numbers not words."

Smith told him, "Read the numbers off to me and then write down what I say once I go into my trance or whatever."

"You'd best sit down first, old man."

Smith took a wicker chair. "Go ahead," he said.

26

A pair of white doves came fluttering down through the waning day, settling in the remains of an arched window in the tumbled down wall of the ruined temple. Smith glanced away from them to look once again down through the darkening forest that covered most of the hillside.

He saw Jennifer at last, climbing up from the pathway below. The oncoming night seemed to be following her, blackening the woodlands in her wake.

Smith forced himself to stay where he was beside the ruined grey stone wall.

"Well, what's on your mind?" she asked when she was still a dozen yards from him.

"You're late. I thought maybe—"

"Benton arrived just after you called," Jennifer told him. "I had to wait until he wasn't with me."

Smith sat on a fallen, moss-streaked column. "There are some things we have to talk over."

"So you mentioned." She sat next to him, stretching

out her legs. "Funny, I never expected we'd be here together again."

The dusk closed in all around them, filling this skeleton of what had been centuries ago the altar room.

"Neither did I," said Smith.

"Jared . . . I really was fond of you back then."

"I know."

"I'm not lying. You and I have always been honest with each other."

"That's not exactly the impression I ended up with."

"You and I could never have had a successful life together. You weren't the sort of man to . . . well, no matter. It's all over and done."

"Not the kind of man to lead a stable, responsible life. That's what your father told me when he suggested I cease forcing my attentions on you."

"Daddy was right, wasn't he? I know what sort of life you've lived the past few—"

"How come he was so certain about my future?"

"He'd worked out a way of testing all you Horizon Kids," replied Jennifer. "When he showed me the results of the tests he'd done with you—"

"That's the reason?" Smith stood. "You did this to me all those years ago because your damn father showed you some projections of what I might turn out—"

"He was right. You screwed up years of your life and there's no reason why I should have—"

"It might not have happened if—"

"What difference does that make now?"

"You loved me. I loved you. But you let that bastard convince you—"

"Don't talk about my father that way." She stood to face him. "And as for loving you . . . I'm not really sure I ever felt anything but . . . well, I hate to say this, Jared, but I was . . . sorry for you mostly."

He took a slow careful breath, then said, "Let's move to other matters."

"That would be better. I really am sorry you've been brooding about this all these—"

"Why didn't you tell me I was one of the ten?"

Jennifer turned away from him. The forest was dark now. "That was Benton's idea," she said. "He wasn't sure you could be trusted, because of what had happened with you and me."

"You told him about that?"

"He's my husband."

"When you warned me to be careful, you could've told me then."

"I wasn't sure of you either."

"So you figured that when I brought in the five missing Horizon Kids, you'd whisper the triggering numbers in my ear," he said. "I'd go obligingly glassyeyed, recite my part of the formula your dear old dad had hidden away in my skull."

"Yes, something like that, yes."

"Games," he said. "You've been trying to play games with me."

"I don't want to remind you that you're working for us," Jennifer said. "And, I must add, you haven't thus far done a very satisfactory job. According to the Whistler Agency reports none of the missing people has been found. Considering the fees paid by Triplan I was expecting—"

"I've got them all."

Jennifer took a step closer to him. "The Horizon Kids? Then why haven't you reported that, turned them over to—"

"Several reasons. I want to keep them alive. Oscar Ruiz, Liz, Winiarsky and me."

"Leaving them off somewhere that Syndek can—"

"Syndek didn't kill Hal Larzon."

"Of course they did. I—"

"Nope. I can prove that."

"There's no one else who could've done anything like that."

"There are at least three people," Smith told her. "Of those three, I'd vote for Benton Arloff, since—"

"Yes, I see." She swung out across the darkness between them, slapping him, hard, across the cheek. "You go into business for yourself, betray mother and me and then try to frame my husband for—"

"Jennifer, it isn't Syndek and it's not the Trinidad Law Bureau," he said evenly. "Now, if your husband could make you all believe that somebody like Syndek was out to trap the secret holders and kill them, he—"

"We already had Larzon's part, before he was killed. So what—"

"He could eventually kill some of the Kids you hadn't reached yet, after he got what he needed," said Smith. "And, most likely, once he'd established the idea that the opposition wasn't above killing, I was the most obvious candidate for that. Actually, I'm not sure he wasn't figuring to kill all of us. That way he'd have the information and there'd be no way for you to get it. To get the transmutation process all to himself—"

"How'd you find out what the secret was?"

"I'm an investigator, remember. I find out things."

Jennifer shook her head. "You're wrong," she said. "We'll go down to Horizon House right now, talk to Benton. He'll convince you."

"No need for that, love," said the tall, thickset man who stepped from behind a slice of ruined temple wall. Even in the new night they could see the silver kilgun in his right hand.

"Benton, why did you follow me?"

"Because, darling," answered her husband, "your old buddy Smith is right about me."

27

Jennifer watched her husband walking toward them. "Benton, I don't understand—"

"No doubt Smith does."

Smith said, "All is better than a third."

"Exactly," said Arloff, smiling at them both.

"But we . . . love each other."

"Later on, love, we can talk about it," her husband said. "Right now, though, I'm going to deprive you of Smith's company."

"You didn't kill Hal Larzon," she said, unsure.

"I did, yes. And for the very reason your clever former beau mentioned." He gestured at Smith with the kilgun. "I'll have to take you someplace where I can persuade you to tell me where the others are."

"I doubt you can accomplish that, Arloff."

Arloff laughed. "Oh, there's not a doubt in my mind," he said. "After that, and after I've gathered in the last bits of the puzzle, then I'll see about arranging some accidents and disappearances for you Horizon Kids.''

Jennifer said quietly, ''You aren't going to kill him, Benton.''

''You actually, darling, don't have a hell of a lot of say in the matter.''

''Benton,'' she said, even more quietly.

That made him turn toward her. ''Really now, Jenny.''

She'd taken a small kilgun from the pocket of her jacket. It was aimed at her husband. ''You'd just,'' she said, ''better go away from here.''

Laughing again, he started easing to her. ''I know you, love,'' he said. ''You can't shoot me, no matter what you think or feel.''

''I won't let you kill Jared.''

''You will because . . . oof.''

Smith had leaped at the distracted Arloff.

The doves went flapping up into the darkness.

As the two men fell Smith got a grip on Arloff's gunwrist. They rolled and tumbled on the stone temple floor.

Grunting, Arloff tried to knee him in the groin.

Smith twisted, avoided that.

The thickset man strained, struggling to regain control of the kilgun. Smith was forced to let go of his wrist for a second, then caught it again.

In that instant the gun went off, sending a thin line of crackling crimson light slicing across the night.

Arloff made a terrible keening sound when the beam touched him. His face began to smoke and go black.

Stumbling back and away, Smith stood.

Arloff made three jerking movements, shoulders and

arms shaking. Then he was dead, smoke rising up from his ruined head.

Bending, Smith picked up the kilgun. He held it gingerly, as though it were dirty.

"You killed him," Jennifer said.

Smith, he had no idea why, grinned. "I wasn't exactly planning to, but—"

"It doesn't matter. Doesn't matter."

He crossed to her, reached out the hand that didn't hold the kilgun. "Jennifer, there's nothing—"

"It's all right, Jared," she said. "But, please, don't touch me. Don't talk to me anymore. Don't follow me." She left him there and went hurrying downhill through the night forest.

Saint rewound the plaid muffler around his neck. The fog was thick and prickly in the quirky lane. "A sad turn of events," he remarked.

Cruz said, "He may not be in this public house either."

"One hopes not, but judging from what Jennifer told us when we called at Horizon House in quest of him, I fear the worst."

Cruz pushed open the sewdooak door of the Snerg & Racket with his metal hand. "I lose the bet, there's Smith yonder."

There were some twenty or so patrons in the snug room, most of them at the small tables ringing the deep blazing fireplace. Two played at airdarts in a far corner.

Smith sat at a table alone, both hands locked around a glass.

"Not that the chap doesn't have a perfect right to backslide under the circumstances," said Saint.

Cruz led the way to Smith. "How're you faring, old chum?"

Smith looked up at him. "It was Arloff," he said. "He's dead, up at the temple ruins. We'll have to notify the local law soon."

Saint rubbed at his nose, frowning down at Smith. "Jove, you're perfectly sober."

"He's drinking sparkling water," said Cruz, seating himself opposite.

"No more binges," said Smith. "That only happened in my youth. And that's over."

"Forgive me for having so little faith." Saint dusted the third chair before sitting.

Smith nodded. "We'd better get back to the satellite," he said, finishing his drink. "I just came in here to warm up. Seems damn chilly out tonight."

"Deucedly so," agreed Saint.

28

From the living room of Smith's hotel suite he could see the stretch of beach where he and Jennifer had walked when he'd first arrived on Zegundo. The afternoon was grey.

Smith was sitting in a plaz slingchair, hunched, chin resting on his steepled fingers.

The voxbox in the room's ceiling made a throatclearing noise before announcing, "An unsavory gentleman with a suspicious moustache and a dangerous right arm is at the door, sire, accompanied by a clinging blonde humanoid young woman."

"Show them in." Smith stretched up out of the chair.

"You're absolutely certain, sire, that you wish to—"

"In, yes."

Cruz had his arm around Jazz Miller's waist. "I return from the meeting with Jennifer and her mother at the Triplan headquarters with glad tidings," he announced.

"Me, I didn't even get to sit in," complained Jazz.

"All these terrific news stories are breaking all about me and I don't even get the chance to—"

"Recline someplace," advised Cruz, letting go of her.

"Calamity," she said. "I was being a nag again, huh?" She took a seat on the lucite sofa.

Smith asked, "They agreed to the terms?"

"You could've attended this confab, Jared. Both the ladies were quite cordial," said Cruz. "Tea was served."

"I wasn't certain Jennifer would want to see me."

"She asked after you."

"Oh, so?"

"I informed her you were pining and sulking here in Suite 1304 of the Selva Plaza."

"And you told her I was leaving the planet at midnight?"

"I managed to mention that, yes." He sat in a tin slingchair. "She knows how to get in touch with you."

"Okay," said Smith, starting to pace. "Are they going to draw up papers and all?"

Cruz nodded. "Yes, although this deal has to remain more or less under the table for now."

"I can't even do a dinky three-minute spot on the news about it," mentioned Jazz, folding her arms under her breasts.

"One million trubux for each of the surviving Horizon Kids and a pro rata share of half the profits?" said Smith.

"They agreed so swiftly, I'm thinking we well might have persuaded them to put up a larger sum in front."

"The deal's okay as it stands."

Rubbing at his metal hand, Cruz said, "You should have your money within a month. That puts you in an entirely different status position, old chum. What do you intend to—"

"Not sure. I'm going back to the Barnum System for

awhile. Haven't figured what'll happen beyond that."

Cruz stood. "This has been a gratifying association, and not merely because of the bonus all you Horizon House grads are bestowing on Saint and myself." He held out his right hand. "Should you want me for any further adventures, you can reach me here on Zegundo."

"Don't go offering him any jobs that are going to get him killed," cautioned Jazz.

Smith and Cruz shook hands.

The pixphone buzzed at a few moments beyond three in the afternoon.

"Might be Jennifer," Smith told himself, striding to the phone alcove in the suite living room. "Hello?"

Saint's green face popped onto the screen. "Jove, you look deuced glum for a chap who's just become rich for life."

"I always look glum on phone screens," Smith told him. "Nothing more than an electronic trick. How are you?"

"Quite content," Saint answered. "As soon as I collect the handsome bonus you tots have bestowed, I'll be embarking for Terzero."

"A job?"

"A baroness. This time, however, a quite lovely lady in her late thirties. She once suggested that should I ever give up my shameful life of crime, she'd like to see more of me."

"Are you reforming?"

"Until the current influx of fortune runs out, at least," Saint said. "Take care and should you ever again have need of an accomplished, not to mention charming, telek, do contact me. I can be reached at the Villa Splendide on Terzero."

"Okay, and good luck."

He returned to his chair and sat watching the ocean far below.

"Hangdog look defined." The floating Whistler terminal materialized a few feet in front of him.

"Move. You're blocking the splendid view."

Staying where it was, the terminal said, "You're not going to go back to wallowing in gutters, are you?"

"Not on my agenda, no."

"Good. You do have a certain potential and you may eventually live up to it."

"Your glowing compliments are always appreciated in this quarter."

"I've come to inform you that there are no hard feelings," said Whistler. "You held up our clients for a bundle, but you also solved the case and did what we were hired to do. So the Whistler organization isn't going to be fuddyduddy about this."

Smith said, "If everybody'd leveled with us from the start, we—"

"No matter. The point is, the outfit is satisfied with you, and your crew. It's possible that in the future we'll call on you again. Interested?"

"Might be. Working for Suicide, Inc. has been great fun."

"We'll meet again." Whistler vanished.

An hour later the pixphone sounded again.

"She'll probably call, if only to say goodbye."

This time it was Deac Constiner. "Hello, nitwit," the Trinidad Law Bureau agent commenced.

"You're very cordial. Do many people compliment you on that qualit—"

"I don't have any proof of this," said Constiner. "But I think you and your goons have sabotaged me and done me physical harm all along the way. Since you're now fleeing the planet, I also assume you've rounded up the remaining Horizon Kids and sold them to your client."

"Did you say you *had* proof? I didn't quite catch—"

"No, you dimwit, I don't have proof." Constiner's leathery face looked like it was rapidly becoming drier. "If I did, your arse would be reposing in the hoosegow at this very moment. Should I ever come up with so much as a scrap, beware."

"I'll be on Barnum for a spell. Can you extradite me from—"

"I'll extradite you from the furthest little pissant planet in the remotest galaxy in this nitwit universe. I'll . . . and, another thing, Smith. I don't believe that flapdoodle about Benton Arloff."

"Which flapdoodle is that, Deac?"

"That he was accidentally killed while hunting."

"Sounds plausible to me. I know the guy was a real gun enthusiast."

"What I don't understand is how come you didn't end up in the sack with the widow."

Smith grinned thinly. "Because I'm a decent, law-abiding fellow." He hung up.

He went back to his chair.

It seemed likely that Jennifer would get in touch with him. He'd been right about her husband, about what had been going on. She ought to realize that by now. He didn't expect an apology, but at least a thank you, a goodbye.

He sat in the room the rest of the day, watching the sea go dark.

But she never called.